Kuils River

D0501461

Strand

Bay

Rooi-Els

To Lavanya—
Always say "I can"!
—Mister Lemur!

ESCAPE TO CAPE TOWN
By Mister Lemur

Published by Ringtail Learning, San Francisco, CA

ISBN: 978-0-9828866-8-7
Library of Congress Control Number: 2015953289

To explore more of The Scheming Lemurs' world, visit
www.MisterLemur.com.

This book is available at a quantity discount when purchased for
educational use. Contact misterlemur@misterlemur.com

Mister Lemur is a trademark of Hans Hartvickson.

Thank you to Amy Bauman and Mimi Lemur for their editorial
insights. We would also like to thank; Snigdha and Gopal for
awesome illustrations and videos. . . the musicians behind the
band, including multi-talented producer and musician Doug "Silky"
Allen who teamed with singer-songwriter Dave "Numbat"
Haberman on *Nature Police, 2043*, and *Rivals in Rhyme*, with Dave
and Lauren Haberman on *Preposition Punk*, and Jonny Williams on
O.R.E.O. . . . Selamawit Alemayehu and Barry Mattson for the song
Yes, I Can. . . and Blake Foss for creating the website where you
can watch the videos and hear the songs.

Manufactured by Thomson-Shore, Dexter, MI (USA); RMA94DK87,
December, 2015

For Karsten,

Dream big dreams and follow them. If you believe in yourself, you can do anything!

ESCAPE TO CAPE TOWN

Lemur Notes: i

Chapter 1: Anywhere but Airborne 1

Chapter 2: Reluctant Rider 4

Chapter 3: Captain Aye-Aye 7

Chapter 4: That's Why I *Never* Eat Cactus 10

Chapter 5: Gone Phishing 17

Chapter 6: Twisted Rickshaws 21

Chapter 7: Hugging in my Junkyard 24

Chapter 8: Totaled in Tow 26

Chapter 9: A Cough That Won't Turn Off 27

Chapter 10: Lemurs at Work 30

Chapter 11: Scheming 33

Chapter 12: Weather Guessers 35

Chapter 13: In Passing 37

Chapter 14: Work Party 42

Chapter 15: Obvious 42

Chapter 16: This Looks Hot! 45

Chapter 17: A Plan in Motion 49

Chapter 18: Escape to Cape Town 55

Chapter 19: Sunset 58

Chapter 20: Unusual.. 61

Chapter 21: Landing? 63

Chapter 22: Let's Table This....................................... 68

Chapter 23: Penguins 70

Chapter 24: Cape Flats.. 74

Chapter 25: The University of Cape Town 78

Chapter 26: Your Futures.. 85

Chapter 27: 2043.. 88

Chapter 28: Results 90

Chapter 29: Silent 93

Chapter 30: The Campus Coffee Corner 95

Chapter 31: Second Chance... 98

Chapter 32: Good News; Bad News 101

Chapter 33: Selam.. 103

Chapter 34: Star Struck 106

Chapter 35: Duct Tape.. 111

Chapter 36: Sunday Morning 113

Chapter 37: Sayonara, Silky? 117

Chapter 38: Finders Weepers..................................... 119

Chapter 39: Theories 123

Chapter 40: Nocturnal by Nature.............................. 125

Chapter 41: Pacing 128

Chapter 42: Nervous Talker 129

Chapter 43: Bellhop Stop 133

Chapter 44: Leftovers.. 136

Chapter 45: Involuntary.. 143

Chapter 46: The Reverse Santa Claus 145

Chapter 47: Directions 155

Chapter 48: A Plan 156

Chapter 49: On Topic 157

Chapter 50: Preposition Punk................................... 164

Chapter 51: Grave Danger 165

Chapter 52: The Envelope, Please............................. 166

Chapter 53: Rodents? 172

Chapter 54: The Back Window 173

Chapter 55: Why? 176

Chapter 56: Closure... 180

Chapter 57: The VBC 185

Lemur Notes:

Have you ever tried to tickle yourself?

Conventional wisdom says that you can't actually tickle yourself. At least, not in that *roll around on the ground laughing until you pee your pants* kind of way.

Try it. I'll wait.

Interesting; right? But I don't like to talk about what we *can't* do. I'm much more into what we *can* do when we put our minds to something. *Escape to Cape Town* is about me putting my mind to becoming the most famous writer in the world. I wrote it trying to tickle my own fancy, which I know is possible. I hope it tickles your fancy, too.

Despite a name that sounds too cool to be true, Cape Town is a real place. Not because everyone wears capes (which *would* be

To tickle someone's fancy: To amuse or entertain someone; to stimulate someone's imagination in a favorable manner

cool!), but because it is located on the Cape of Good Hope, on the south-western most point of the continent of Africa.

My name is Oliver Lemur, and, as I explained before, I'm trying to become the most famous writer in the world.

I think I'm a really good writer, but most adults don't want to take me seriously. For one thing, I'm a ring-tailed lemur. Adults are always telling me, "We already have lots of good books *for* people written *by* people. Why don't you write books for lemurs?"

The other thing working against me is that I'm still in elementary school. When I tell adults that I'm a writer, they usually pat me on the head and say, "That's so cute!"

This book is part two of my quest to win the world-renowned "Rivals in Rhyme" writing contest. I'll explain the specific rules later, but for now, just know that you win Rivals in

PASSPORT NO./NO DU PASSEPORTE
086421231

Surname / Nom
LEMUR

Given names / Prénoms
OLIVER

Nationality / Nationalité
MADAGASCAR

Date of birth / Date de naissance
21 / OCT

Place of birth / Lieu di naissance
RANAMOFANA

Sex / Sexe
M

Species/ especies
LEMUR CATTA

Instruments/Instruments
BASS

Mister Lemur

SIGNATURE OF BEARER / SIGNATURE DU TITULAIRE

Oliver Lemur is a ring-tailed lemur from Ranomafana National Park in southeastern Madagascar. He is very creative and loves to write stories and songs. Oliver believes he is the best writer in the world, and is determined to show his talent to the world. He lives with his mother and father, his sister Lemur Pup, and his dog Henry. He attends Ranomoura Elementary School. Oliver plays the bass guiter, and likes to be known by his pen name, "Mister Lemur." In addition to speaking Lemur, Mister Lemur speaks Malagasy (the language of Madagascar natives), English, and some French.

P<RTLLEMUR<<OLIVER<<<<<<<<<<<<<<<<<<<<<
086421231RTL20101101M1006113<<<<<<<<<<<<<<

Rhyme by convincing the judges that your team is the wittiest writer of riddles, raps, or rhyming poems in the contest.

Rivals in Rhyme is a big, multi-round event, and a team must win three local and regional competitions to advance to the world finals.

Our first round was the Country Competition, where we competed against all the other teams from our home country of Madagascar. You can read about that in Book One of this series, which is called *The Scheming Lemurs; Rivals in Rhyme*.

You are now reading Book Two, which is the story of the Continent Competition, where we compete against the top teams from all the other countries that make up the continent of Africa.

The top teams from each Continent Competition advance to one of the Hemisphere Competitions.

Finally, the teams with the strongest performances in the Hemisphere Competitions (Northern and Southern) advance to the World Finals.

So as you can see, Rivals in Rhyme is a big deal… and a great opportunity to show everyone that the best writer in the world is right here at Ranomafana's Namorana Elementary! (That's me!)

Speaking of me, this is probably a good time to explain why I have two names.

Even though the front cover says my name is Mister Lemur, my real name is Oliver. Like a lot of writers, I write under a made-up name, called a "pen name." So "Mister Lemur" is my pen name. I think the

"Mister" part makes me sound older.

If you have not given yourself a pen name yet, I highly recommend you do.

Let me introduce you to my teammates in The Scheming Lemurs, who will be joining us on this fancy-tickling journey:

PASSPORT NO./NO DU PASSEPORTE
97531246

Surname / Nom
SIFAKA

Given names / Prénoms
DOUGLAS

Nationality / Nationalité
MADAGASCAR

Date of birth / Date de naissance
30 / NOV

Place of birth / Lieu di naissance
MAROJEJY

Sex / Sexe
M

Species/ especies
PROPITHECUS
CANDIDUS

Instruments/Instruments
DRUMS/VOCALS

SIGNATURE OF BEARER / SIGNATURE DU TITULAIRE

Douglas "Silky" Sifaka is a silky sifaka lemur from Marojejy (MAR-oh-JAY-gee) National Park in northern Madagascar. In the trees, Sifaka lemurs move by swinging nimbly between branches and vines. On the ground, sifakas move by "dancing" sideways. A master musician, Silky is both the band's drummer and studio engineer/recorder. Rarely seen without his signature "Silky Sunglasses," Silky is the most fashionable member of the group. Sadly, like all silky sifaka lemurs, Douglas is endangered.

P<RTLSIFAKA<<DOUGLAS<<<<<<<<<<<<<<<<<<<<<<<
97531246RTL201009171M1006113<<<<<<<<<<<<<<<<<

PASSPORT NO./NO DU PASSEPORTE
086421254

Surname / Nom
HART

Given names / Prénoms
JENNY

Nationality / Nationalité
U.S.A.

Date of birth / Date de naissance
13 / APR

Place of birth / Lieu di naissance
ANGELS CAMP, CA

Sex / Sexe
F

Species/ especies
HOMO SAPIEN

Instruments/Instruments
KEYBOARD /
VOCALS

Jenny

SIGNATURE OF BEARER / SIGNATURE DU TITULAIRE

Jenny is from the town of Angels Camp, California, a former gold rush town in the foothills of the Sierra Nevada mountains. Jenny took piano lessons from an early age and sang regularly with her church and school. Jenny's mother is a teacher and her father is a musician. Jenny has traveled to 35 different countries and every continent except Antarctica. Jenny is also an illustrator and painter. When not touring with the band, Jenny can be found visiting schools and sharing her love of music, writing and creativity!

P<RTLHART<<JENNY<<<<<<<<<<<<<<<<<<<<<<
086421254RTL19770413M1006113<<<<<<<<<

PASSPORT NO./NO DU PASSEPORTE
97531246

Surname / Nom

Given names / Prénoms
NUMBAT

Nationality / Nationalité
AUSTRALIA

Date of birth / Date de naissance
05 / May

Place of birth / Lieu di naissance
CHERRY TREE POOL

Sex / Sexe
M

Species/ especies
MYRMECOBIUS
FASCIATUS

Instruments/Instruments
GUITAR / VOCALS

Numbat

SIGNATURE OF BEARER / SIGNATURE DU TITULAIRE

Numbat is a banded anteater from the town of Cherry Tree Pool in Western Australia. Born beside a billabong to a family of farmers, Numbat began playing music at the age of two. His musical style was shaped by countless hours jamming with aboriginal children and local indigenous animals such as quokka, wallabies, and rufous treecreepers. Numbat's pursuit of music took him from Cherry Tree Pool to Sydney, on the eastern coast of Australia, and eventually, to Madagascar. He used to have a name, but someone actually wore it out, so now people just call him Numbat. That works, since he's the only numbat in Ranomafana National Park.

P<RTLNUMBAT<<NUMBAT<<<<<<<<<<<<<<<<<
97531246RTL99<<<<<<<<<<<<<<<<<<<<<<<

I have recorded the events of this story as accurately as I can recall them. In some cases, I pieced together parts of the story through interviews. In others cases, I reconstructed parts from the journals of those involved after the adventure was over. I don't want to give too much away, but as you will see, these journals revealed that some of those who I thought were my friends were really not so friendly!

Because I want you to enjoy my books, I always think about why I'm writing. Writers call this "the author's purpose." Authors write to persuade, inform, or entertain (P.I.E.!). In this book I'm writing to entertain you, but I also hope the story of my adventure will persuade you that I'm the best writer in the world!

You'll also see that I've created some videos and songs to help me tell this story. At various times in this book, I will suggest that you use a bookmark to keep your place while you go to the Internet to watch videos of some scenes and hear some songs. At each of these places, you will see directions on what to do.

SEE ONE OF THESE?

Follow the link online to access music, photos, videos and blogs that accompany the story.

Oh, and if this book does (or does not) tickle your fancy, feel free to e-mail me and tell me why.

My e-mail is <u>misterlemur@misterlemur.com</u>

We begin this story flying back to our home village of Ranomafana from Madagascar's capital city of Tana. We were in Tana trying to raise money for the trip to Cape Town for the "All Africa" Continent Competition round of Rivals in Rhyme.

PASSPORT NO./NO DU PASSEPORTE
17674370

Surname / Nom
VON BLAKE

Given names / Prénoms
BARON

Nationality / Nationalité
FRENCH

Date of birth / Date de naissance
DECEMBER 30

Place of birth / Lieu di naissance
LA RÉUNION

Sex / Sexe
M

Species/ especies
HOMO SAPIEN

Instruments/Instruments
DRUMS

The Baron

SIGNATURE OF BEARER / SIGNATURE DU TITULAIRE

In a national park full of characters, Baron Von Blake might be the most unusual. He can often be found talking about his pet enchilada. It is rumored that his favorite food is pickle pancakes. There is also significant doubt whether he really is a baron. As the story goes, his great, great, great grandfather held several very important positions with the government when Madagascar was a French colony. This was a long time ago—Madagascar was a French colony from 1897 to 1960. He claims that this great, great, great grandfather was French nobility, and that this lineage—this family history—makes him a baron. After 1960, his family fled to the French island of La Réunion, where The Baron was born.

P<RTLVONBLAKE,BARON<<BARON<<<<<<<<<<<<<<<<
17674370RTL189721960C15<<<<<<<<<<<<<<<<<<<<

Chapter 1: Anywhere but Airborne

SUNDAY
February
02

The more I flew with The Baron, the less I liked flying. Our whole band had been crammed into his mail plane for two turbulent hours, and we were ready to be anywhere but airborne.

At long last, the familiar outline of the Ranomoura River appeared below us, and The Baron eased the throttle slightly. The twin engines on his vintage DC-2

Somewhere over Ranomafana National Park, Madagascar

mellowed, and we began an unusually rapid descent.

"Dude! You late for something?!" Numbat cracked.

But The Baron didn't laugh.

"Oh la Vache!" **he gasped. "Zeat belt! Zeat belt! Every vun a zeat belt!"**

He pulled his aviator goggles dramatically over his eyes.

We scrambled to strap ourselves into "zeat belts," hurriedly pushing loads of letters and piles of postcards from our seats.

Silky—the most fashion-forward member of the band—rushed to secure his two overflowing orange suitcases, clutching them tightly as he fumbled at his seat belt. Before I

Oh la Vache! is a French expression similar to "Holy cow!"

heard a successful click, I heard an ear-splitting

THWaaaaaaaaaPP. . . thhhhhhhhhhhhhhhhhhhhhhhh . . . CRACK!!

as the plane belly flopped violently into the mud and slid down the soggy riverbank. It must have looked like a banana dropped from a third-story window onto a steeply sloped ice skating rink . . . if you can picture that.

A blizzard of letters filled the air inside the mail plane, covering everything—and everyone. We all screamed.

Except Silky.

Chapter 2: Reluctant Rider

I looked around the wrecked plane in wide-eyed amazement. Letters and postcards fluttered to the floor around me. I saw The Baron and Jenny sitting in the front seats, frantically flipping switches to turn off anything that could start a fire. The main door had come off, and the left wing was mostly gone. The whole tail of the plane—where Silky was sitting—had detached.

Silky's seat was empty, and his seatbelt hung limply on his seat. His two orange suitcases had tumbled from the plane, which was now resting only a few precarious feet from the bank of the Ranomoura River. The frothy water raged beside what was left of the wing, sweeping logs and branches wildly downstream.

I snapped out of my seat belt and bounded toward the water. "Silky!? Silky!?"

A flash of orange caught my eye downstream. The larger of Silky's two large suitcases bobbed through the rapids, bumping against rocks and gliding through riffles. Silky sat atop his bobbing bag like a terribly miscast bull rider, reluctantly riding a bull that only fashion designer Louis Vuitton could love.

"Jump! Jump to shore!" I screamed. "There's a waterfall!"

He was only a few feet from the river's edge, but Silky wouldn't dismount. He batted feebly at the water, trying to paddle his prized case toward the riverbank.

"Juuuuuump!"

An instant before he would have crashed over the waterfall, Silky sprang from his suitcase, landing colorfully on the rocky shore. He looked like a well-dressed wet dog, but he was okay.

PASSPORT NO./NO DU PASSEPORTE
086421231

Surname / Nom
LEMUR
Given names / Prénoms
OLIVER
Nationality / Nationalité
MADAGASCAR
Date of birth / Date de naissance
21 / OCT
Place of birth / Lieu di naissance
RANOMAFANA

Sex / Sexe
M
Species/ especies
LEMUR CATTA
Instruments/Instruments
BASS

Sex / Sexe
M
Species/ especi
MYRMECOBI
FASCIATUS
Instruments/In
GUITAR/

PASSPORT NO./NO DU PASSEPORTE
122575023

Surname / Nom
AYE-AYE
Given names / Prénoms
CAPTAIN
Nationality / Nationalité
MADAGASCAR
Date of birth / Date de naissance
10/DEC
Place of birth / Lieu di naissance
RANOMAFANA

Sex / Sexe
M
Species/ especies
D.MADAGASCARINESIS
Instruments/Instruments
VOCALS

Captain Aye-Aye

SIGNATURE OF BEARER / SIGNATURE DU TITULAIRE

Captain Aye Aye is the head of the Ranomafana branch of The Nature Police. Before becoming an officer, he was a pilot in the Madagascar Air Force. His call sign was "The Robin" and he is still very fond of the nickname to this day. Like all aye-aye lemurs, Captain Aye-Aye is nocturnal, meaning he is active at night and usually sleeps during the day. He is the subject of the popular song, "The Nature Police" by The Scheming Lemurs.

P<RTLAYEAYE,CAPTAIN<<CAPTAINAYEAYE<<<<<<<<<<<<
122575023RTL8675309771315<<<<<<<<<<<<<<<<<<<<<<<<<

SIGNATURE OF BEARER / SIGNATURE DU TI

In a national park full of characters, Baron Von Blake
unusual. He can often be found talking about his pet enchil
is rumored that his favorite food is pickle pancakes. There is also
significant doubt whether he really is a baron. As the story goes,
his great, great, great grandfather held several very important
positions with the government when Madagascar was a French colony.
This was a long time ago—Madagascar was a French colony from 1897
to 1960. He claims that this great, great, great grandfather was French
nobility, and that this lineage—this family history—makes him a baron.
1960 his family fled to the French island of La Réunion, where

Chapter 3: Captain Aye-Aye

MONDAY
February

03

FEBRUARY
SU MO TU WE TH FR SA
                    1
2 3 4 5 6 7 8
9 10 11 12 13 14 15
16 17 18 19 20 21 22
23 24 25 26 27 28

The circumstances of the crash certainly seemed suspicious, so we decided to report the incident to the police.

After knocking on the nondescript metal door to the office labeled "Nature Police" for five minutes, I finally turned the knob. The door swung open with a loud *creak* to reveal a pitch-black room. I flipped the light switch. An old bulb, hanging from the ceiling by a ratty cord, crackled softly before filling the room with gentle yellow light.

Captain Aye-Aye, the head of Ranomafana's Nature Police, sat up in his chair and put his hands over his eyes. Other than the captain, his desk, chair, and light, the room was completely empty.

Captain Aye-Aye never drank coffee in the morning, for fear that it would keep him awake all day.

"Captain Aye-Aye, we're here to report a very suspicious string of bad luck," I began.

"YOU WANT TO REPORT *BAD LUCK*? THERE'S NO LAW AGAINST . . ."

Jenny jumped in. "What Oliver is trying to say is that we've had a very suspicious set of things happen to us over the last few months. It could be just bad luck, but it seems like something more . . . sinister."

I resumed, "The Ranomafana National Park police told us this matter was out of their jurisdiction, as this is likely 'animal-on-animal' crime. They suggested we speak to you, the Nature Police."

When I finished, Captain Aye-Aye closed his eyes and exhaled deeply. He sat silently for a long moment. We watched him expectantly, trying to read his body language.

"Dude! I think he's asleep," Numbat finally whispered.

He was.

Aye-aye lemurs are nocturnal, which means they are active at night and they sleep

---

Jurisdiction: An area where someone or something has the official power to make legal decisions and judgments all day. This arrangement has some advantages for a detective, but some serious disadvantages for someone trying to talk with him at ten in the morning.

We explained the full situation to Captain Aye-Aye when he awoke—asking him lots of questions along the way and talking really LOUDLY so he stayed awake. He promised to investigate, starting that very night.

"BUT, BASED ON WHAT YOU'VE EXPLAINED," he warned. **"I'D START TO KEEP YOUR . . . PLANS . . . TAWWW . . . *ZZZZZZZZZ.*"**

MisterLemur.com/CT10

- Hear the song *Nature Police*, featuring Captain Aye-Aye (call sign: The Robin) by the Scheming Lemurs (this is one of my favorite songs)

Chapter 4: That's Why I *Never* Eat Cactus

It was our southern hemisphere summer, and Namorana Elementary School was closed for break. In the weeks since we'd finished the Rivals in Rhyme: Madagascar competition, I'd been busy with my friends writing stories and songs at my favorite summer camp, called Adventures in Writing Camp.

For one of our camp projects, Numbat and I decided to write a theme song for Rivals in Rhyme. We made a plan to record it, then sell copies as a way to raise money for the trip to Cape Town.

I'll share our rough draft.

RIVALS IN RHYME
   By Numbat and Mister Lemur

If you want to change the world
here's your opportunity
to create a world of your own,
in books and on TV.

Let your imagination carry you,
to anything you want to be
when you become a character,
for all the world to see.

Put your pen to paper
Rivals in Rhyme, Rivals in Rhyme,
invent a world of your own,
one adventure at a time.

Rivals in Rhyme, Rivals in Rhyme,
make sure to bring your best,
with every single line.
Rivals in Rhyme

Every song you've ever heard,
began inside a writer's head
Every line in every movie
that every character has said

Who will write the next amazing book
that everybody's read?
It could be Mister Lemur,
or it could be you instead!
Rivals in Rhyme

MisterLemur.com/CT13

- Hear a recording of Numbat and Mister Lemur's song, *Rivals in Rhyme*

PASSPORT NO./NO DU PASSEPORTE
22904447

Surname / Nom
LIN

Given names / Prénoms
TAMBO

Nationality / Nationalité
MADAGASCAR

Date of birth / Date de naissance
JANUARY 17

Place of birth / Lieu di naissance
RANOMAFANA

Sex / Sexe
M

Species/ especies
VARECIA VARIEGATA

Instruments/Instruments
TAMBOURINE

Tambo

SIGNATURE OF BEARER / SIGNATURE DU TITULAIRE

Tambo (pronounced "Tam –Bo", like a tambourine) is a black-and -white ruffed lemur from Ranomafana. He is the owner of The Vanilla Bean Café, a favorite hang out for tourists and locals alike in the park. Tambo's banana split is famously good, and is the most popular item on his menu. Tambo is a retired author and songwriter, and a very talented "word-smith." He is one of the older lemurs in the park, and is one of the best dressed as well. You will typically find Tambo wearing slacks, dress shoes, a dress shirt with rolled up sleeves, a necktie, and a fedora style hat.

P<RTLLIN,TAMBO<<TAMBO<<<<<<<<<<<<<<
22904447RTL22202HOH41377<<<<<<<<<<<<<<<<<<

SIGNATURE OF BEARER /

In a national park full of characters, ba unusual. He can often be found talking about is rumored that his favorite food is pickle pancakes. significant doubt whether he really is a baron. As the story goes, his great, great, great grandfather held several very important positions with the government when Madagascar was a French colony. This was a long time ago–Madagascar was a French colony from 1897 to 1960. He claims that this great, great, great grandfather was French nobility, and that this lineage–this family history–makes him a baron. after 1960, his family fled to the French island of La Réunion, where

Every day after camp, I'd sit at the counter of the Vanilla Bean Café ("The VBC") with my notebook in hand while Tambo, the owner, served as my writing coach.

When a customer came in, Tambo would pause to make them one of his famous banana splits or perhaps a hot cocoa with local Madagascar vanilla.

Numbat was sitting next to me, and we were eating ice cream and reviewing our draft of the Rivals in Rhyme song. As soon as we finished one round of banana splits, we ordered another.

Tambo looked at us hesitantly. "You KNOW what they always SAY: 'You are what you eat.'"

Numbat looked back at Tambo. "I always say: 'You poop what you eat.'"

"Ahem, well, yes . . ."

Numbat licked the last of the ice cream from his fingers. "That's why I never eat cactus."

Chapter 5: Gone Phishing

"Dudes! Check it out! You're not going to believe our luck!" Numbat blurted as we gathered for band practice.

"So I got this crazy e-mail this morning from this prince dude in Nigeria that I've never met before. He has a mongo fortune tied up in a bank account in some other random country—I think he said 'Hazmatistan.' He just needed ten thousand dollars to be able to pay someone—, uh, 'trusty'—to get to the money. Then he said he was going to give us a quarter of the fortune for helping him out of a tight spot! We'll be flying to Cape Town in our own private jets. Like, jets *plural*. one for each of us!"

Jenny's eyes got so wide that her eyebrows almost

touched her ears. "You didn't actually send him any money. Did you?"

"oh, for sure! Prince Dude said he needed the money today, and he didn't know who else to turn to. I figured we could help the dude out, and we would REALLY help ourselves out. Not to mention that now I'm gonna be 'boys' with a prince. It's a win-win; you know?"

As you might imagine, it was actually a lose-lose for us. Numbat's "kind act" cost us most of the money in the band's bank account, which meant we didn't have enough money to pay for either plane tickets to get to Cape Town, or a hotel room once we got there.

We were all angry, frustrated, and upset. But none of us was shocked. I think we were mostly mad at ourselves for giving Numbat access to the bank account in the first place.

With the next round less than four weeks away, we needed to think of something fast or I was going to miss out on my dream of becoming the most famous writer in the world!

Chapter 6: Twisted Rickshaws

Numbat felt terrible, and he was determined to make it up to us. "So, dudes—get this. I'm boys with the dude who runs the scrap yard in Ambatovory. I scoop old metal from him for projects. I'll bet I can turn some of the junk there into a drum kit, mic stands, a stand for the keyboard. We can sell some of it and make back the money."

It seemed like the best idea we had going.

"Sure, whatever tickles your fancy."

So that afternoon, Numbat, Silky, and I biked to the junkyard. When Numbat's buddy Zoma opened the gate to the yard, we set out walking through the many rows piled high with old car frames, rusty refrigerators, and old pieces of railroad track. It was like a toy store for a kid who had grown up to be a

mechanic, and it was a particularly cool place for curious lemurs and friends to explore.

Soon Numbat had wandered off one way, I had gone another, and Silky had taken yet a third direction. I found a metal box that looked as if it would make a great body for a bass guitar, and I had started to look around for something to use as a guitar neck. I was really enjoying—

Aaaaggghhhh!!! AaagghhhHHHH!

I dropped my discovery and began running toward the sound of Silky's freak-out. I could only imagine that his tail was stuck in a refrigerator door or he had fallen into an old toilet, or . . .

The yelling was coming from the very back of the junkyard. As I rounded a big heap of twisted rickshaws, I immediately saw why silky was screaming.

Rickshaw: a light two-wheeled hooded vehicle drawn by one or more people

Chapter 7: Hugging in my Junkyard

There, resting by the back gate, larger than life, was the skeleton of The Baron's wrecked mail plane.

As soon as Silky saw the wreck, memories of the crash came flooding back to him, and his post-traumatic stress disorder (PTSD) had kicked in.

I did the only thing I could think of. I gave him a big lemur hug (using both arms and my tail) and told him he was going to be alright.

We had just commenced our lemur embrace when Numbat and the confused junkyard owner came careening around that same pile of rickshaws. Their expressions could not have been more different.

Zoma had a wide-eyed look of panic that asked "What happened? Is everyone okay?

Careening: to move swiftly and in an uncontrolled way in a specified direction

Why are these lemurs hugging in my junkyard?"

Numbat had a very different expression . . . an inspired smile and eyes that revealed, "I have an idea . . ."

Chapter 8: Totaled in Tow

The Baron's plane was totaled—that is—so badly damaged that it was cheaper for the insurance company to buy him a new one than to pay people to fix the first one. But Numbat saw something in the wreck and haggled Zoma into selling it to him for $50. My first thought was that this was going to be Numbat's second terrible money decision of the day. But he was so excited and had so much conviction in his voice that I kept my mouth shut.

As we were about to leave, Numbat turned to Zoma and started whispering.

"I'll need you to tow it somewhere for me. I'll come back tomorrow and tell you where. Just don't let anything happen to it overnight, and don't mention this conversation to anyone."

Chapter 9: A Cough That Won't Turn Off

Tambo had been home sick for several days straight, and I started to get worried. It took something really serious to keep Tambo out of The VBC for even *one* day, so I decided to drop by his house on my way home.

When I arrived, Tambo's wife, Manda Lin, greeted me with a cup of vanilla tea.

"Tambo is too tired to see visitors, but he left you a note on the kitchen table."

I worriedly picked up Tambo's note. It was, of course, written in rhyme . . . with a note saying "A-B-C-B rhyme scheme, 8-6-8-6 syllable pattern" scribbled across the top. Tambo never missed a chance to mentor me. I know that will totally tickle his fancy when I become the most famous writer in the world.

Oliver,
I've got a cough that won't turn off,
inside my lungs and throat.
And I believe, if it won't leave,
this might be, "all she wrote."

There's windburn on my uvula.
My trachea is sore.
My respiratory system says
it cannot take much more.

My lungs sent me a note that read,
 "Please bring in more physicians.
We do not think that we can work
in these sorts of conditions."

This cough is most unwelcome.
It won't cease; it won't desist.
I've tried to keep an open mind,
but we can't co-exist.

And since this cough will not turn off
or pause or mute or cease,
I'll likely still be coughing when
there's Middle-Eastern peace.

A coughing fit is coming on,
and so, I'd best sign off.
But one last thing I'll say to you-
"Cough cough, Cough Cough, cough, COUGH!

—Tambo

I felt my hands shaking as I read the note, and then I read it again. As I biked home from Tambo's house, I nearly started crying. I couldn't imagine losing Tambo. In addition to being my mentor, he's a great friend and an inspiration. I really wanted him to be okay, and to be around to see me become the world's most famous writer.

Chapter 10: Lemurs at Work

Numbat had Zoma tow (drag, really) the plane to a remote, densely wooded patch of jungle five miles from town. He also bought some smaller pieces of scrap metal—refrigerator doors, old car parts, a piece of an old train car. Then Numbat convinced Zoma to loan him a welding torch and a generator.

Heeding Captain Aye-Aye's warning, we didn't tell anyone about the location of the plane, or that there even WAS a plane. We mapped out secret trails along hard-to-follow routes and moved carefully in and out of the clearing to avoid leaving footprints.

For the next three weeks Numbat barely slept, spending almost every minute he wasn't in camp working on the plane. Fortunately, he was really handy with tools. But to rebuild an entire airplane in three weeks, and to get it to a point where it could make an eight-hour flight over the ocean? That was a lot to ask.

Not to mention that he had to learn to fly.

We used some of the money we had left to rent a large fuel storage tank. Zoma quietly delivered it to the project site, and we used it to fuel the generator. Eventually we'd use it to gas the plane as well . . . if everything went according to plan.

On Captain Aye-Aye's suggestion, we told everyone—especially our rivals Foosana and Lava—that we had tickets to Cape Town on Madagascar's national airline, Air Mad.

PASSPORT NO./NO DU PASSEPORTE
096521244

Surname / Nom
FOOSA

Given names / Prénoms
FOOSANA

Nationality / Nationalitè
MADAGASCAR

Date of birth / Date de naissance
05/OCT

Place of birth / Lieu di naissance
RANOMAFANA

Sex / Sexe
F

Species/ especies
FOSSA FOSSANA

Instruments/Instruments
VOCALS

(signature) Foosana

SIGNATURE OF BEARER / SIGNATURE DU TITULAIRE

Foosana is a singer/songwriter from Ranomafana National Park in Madagascar. As a musician, she has followed in the footsteps of her father Snarlton, who was a talented (if not commercially successful) composer of traditional Malagasy music. Foosana wants desperately to become a famous musician, and her ruthless drive to achieve this goal has left her with few close friends other than Lava, the leaf gecko. She is the founder and lead singer of the band Mrs. Foosa.

P<RTLFOOSANA<<FOOSA<<<<<<<<<<<<<<<<<<<<<<
086421254RM1006113<<<<<<<<<<<<<<<<<<

PASSPORT NO./NO DU PASSEPORTE
99051711

Surname / Nom
CLANDESTINO

Given names / Prénoms
LAVA

Nationality / Nationalitè
MADAGASCAR

Date of birth / Date de naissance
JUNE 15

Place of birth / Lieu di naissance
RANOMAFANA

Sex / Sexe
M

Species/ especies
UROPLATUS

Instruments/Instruments
NONE

(signature) Lava

SIGNATURE OF BEARER / SIGNATURE DU TITULAIRE

Lava is a leaf-tailed gecko from Ranomafana. He is usually green, unless he has changed colors to blend into the environment around him. Like all leaf-tailed geckos, his tail looks remarkably like a tree leaf, making him particularly good at disguising himself. He has eyes that look in two different directions, but he is always looking out for himself first and foremost. Lava enjoys using his hiding ability to spy on others, and he likes to cause trouble. He is often seen absconding with unsupervised ice-cream cones or loose change. Foosa is the only resident of Ranomafana he counts as a friend.

P<RTLCLANDESTINO,LAVA<<LAVA<<<<<<<<<<<<<<<
99051711RTL18191101B8314508 <<<<<<<<<<<<<<<<

Chapter 11: Scheming

Nearly three weeks later

We were too busy over those three weeks to notice that *we'd* been noticed.

"Those Scheming Lemurs are scheming again," Foosana hissed, as she watched Silky and me bike away from The VBC. She'd seen us whispering over milkshakes and seen us sneak out The VBC's back door.

She looked at Lava. "Follow them, and see what they are scheming about. I don't want any surprises.

"Actually, I don't want them in Cape Town at all. But I definitely don't want any surprises."

Chapter 12: Weather Guessers

The airplane repairs were coming along, but the plane's interior was still completely bare. One of the two engines was working, and the other was getting very close.

Numbat pulled me aside Tuesday morning before Adventures in Writing Camp. He'd been wearing a cape to camp for the last several days in excitement about the upcoming trip. I tried to tell him that not everyone in Cape Town wears capes, but he didn't want to listen . . . and I didn't really want to burst his bubble.

"Dude. So get this. The Weather Guessers have changed up the forecast on us. At first they were saying it would stay all dry until Friday, but now it's going to start dumping Wednesday. As in, mañana. We totally need to get the electrical work wrapped today and get tarps up on everything else. I'm calling a work party for this afternoon."

I hesitated. "I'll be there, but I'll be late."

Chapter 13: In Passing

Tambo had been to The VBC only twice since my visit to his home, and both times he looked thin and seemed in pain. I wanted to lift his spirits, and I'd told his wife Manda Lin that I'd come back after camp to visit. I was determined to keep my word, and I really hoped he'd feel like talking to me. I brought a new poem I'd been working on to share, and I knew that would make him happy.

Numbat asked to come with me. He claimed he was worried about Tambo, too, but I think he was mainly worried I would stay there too long instead of helping on the plane.

When we arrived, Tambo's house was dark and quiet. I knocked softly on the screen door to their screened-in patio but heard nothing. I opened the door as quietly as I could, which really wasn't very quietly at all.

SQUEEEEAAK!

A flock of birds took flight from a nearby ficus tree, startling me even more than I'd startled them. I exhaled.

The patio was a simple area with tree stumps carved into lemur-sized chairs and tables.

A bowl of chips sat atop a large round stump-table in the middle of the patio, and Numbat went there directly. I continued to the house door and knocked again.

I waited thirty seconds, but there was no response.

I looked back at Numbat and the chips and saw a series of handwritten pages of binder paper sitting near the bowl. A note on top of the first page in Tambo's wife's handwriting read "Tambo wanted to you to have these." I picked the first one up and saw they were lesson plans with writing tips he'd created for me. I smiled. Even when he was feeling terrible, he was still such a thoughtful—

I froze, and my heart started pounding. I started to feel dizzy. I had finally noticed the second note—just a few rapidly-written words on a carelessly torn piece of paper.

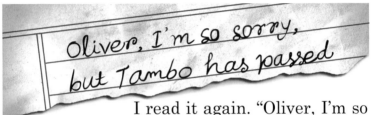

I read it again. "Oliver, I'm so sorry, but Tambo has passed."

The next hour was a blur, but I remember crying a lot. I also remember wanting to do something, but feeling helpless. I started running away from the house. Numbat let me go at first, and then he started chasing me. Confused, I ran back to the house. I grabbed the notes and the lesson plans and stuffed them in my backpack. Then I biked as fast as I could to the work site, even more determined to win the contest and dedicate my first worldwide bestseller to Tambo.

Chapter 14: Work Party

The inside of the plane was really coming together. While Numbat was finishing the second engine, Jenny, Silky, and I were decorating the DC-2's cabin with all the comforts of a small, flying home.

The walls were covered in strands of Christmas lights, and Silky hung a rotating disco ball from the ceiling. One hundred blinking Christmas lights reflected off the mirrored disco ball, casting a thousand moving specs of light around the cabin. A pair of ratty, mismatched couches was tucked against the sidewalls, with rudimentary seatbelts attached. Toward the back, a giant spring, a small metal barrel, and a pony saddle had come together to form a "mechanical bull."

"Numbat installed it for turbulence rodeos," Jenny quipped. "In case we hit more potholes in the sky!"

Chapter 15: Obvious

 From his perch in a ficus tree, Lava watched Foosana spryly climb up to his branch. Once she was situated, they looked down at the construction site below.

Lava stated the obvious. "They didn't, uh, make themselves very, um, hard to find."

Foosana smiled. *"They should have been more careful. I just spoke with some struggling farmers on the edge of town. I reminded the farmers that there is a nice, flat, unclaimed piece of land here that would be perfect for farming. Perfect—that is—if it did not have all this jungle growth.*

"I let them know it was supposed to rain starting Friday, so, Thursday morning, when we're in Tana taxiing down the runway on our Air Mad flight to Cape Town, the local farmers will start a

controlled burn to clear this whole area to plant crops. They don't know that there is an airplane hidden just north of the clearing, and I'm certainly not going to tell them.

"When The Scheming Lemurs come to make final preparations on their plane after camp Thursday—the day after tomorrow—they will find nothing but a burned hunk of metal!

"And, since the next commercial flight to Cape Town after ours is not until Saturday afternoon, they won't arrive by the start of the contest!"

Lava smiled and wrinkled his sensitive nose. "I can, um, almost smell the smoke just, uh, thinking about it!"

Chapter 16: This Looks Hot!

Numbat had been outside working on the second engine for several hours, and he had not seen the transformation of the interior. We knew he was going to be amped. When he finally scampered up the boarding stairs and looked inside the plane, he was wide-eyed. "Dude! This place is on fire!"

Jenny smiled. Silky proudly puffed his hairy chest so much that a button nearly popped right off his orange shirt. "Thanks man. None of this would have been possible without—"

"No, dudes—I mean this place—this part of the forest—is literally on fire. We've gotta bounce out of here!"

We looked out the left side window—then the front window—then the back window. We didn't see fire, but we saw smoke drifting toward us from all directions.

"Wait here!" I yelled, bounding out of the plane. I sprinted out of the clearing, into the forest, and up the tallest tree I could find.

When I got to the top, I saw a wall of fire approaching on all sides, leaving an eerie perimeter of dense white smoke around us. "Field burn? Right now?" I whispered in disbelief.

As forest dwellers, we were familiar with the practice of field burning, where farmers burn an area of jungle to clear land for farming. These burns have devastating effects on all of us who live in the forest. Ranomafana National Park is protected, but to find a secret, remote place that was also flat, Numbat set our repair area outside the park.

It never occurred to us that this might happen.

Despite our recent dry days, the jungle plants were still very wet, so the fire moved slowly, producing a lot of hissing and popping as the wet wood and wet vines burned. This gave off an immense amount of white smoke.

With all the noise and all the smoke, I doubted anyone would be able to hear our calls for help. Not that there was much they could do even if they did hear us.

Chapter 17: A Plan in Motion

I ping-ponged out of the tree and started back to the plane. Before I could reach our worksite, the plane reached me. Jenny was driving while Numbat and Silky darted back and forth swinging machetes to clear vines and limbs from her path.

"Help me move this log!" Numbat yelled.

"We're surrounded! It's a field——"

"We know!" Numbat interrupted. "We're going to fly out!"

"What? Have you checked the engines? The brakes? The——"

"Stop talking and start helping!" Silky screamed. His terrified eyes were almost as large as the rims on his orange "Silky Sunglasses." "We're almost to the clearing!"

He was right, and I did. I'd seen enough from my jaunt up the tree to know this was probably our only chance, even as risky as it was.

We made good progress for another twenty feet, until the tip of the plane's wing clipped the trunk of a tall ficus tree. Normally, hitting a ficus this large would have seriously damaged the plane's wing. However, the ground around the tree's roots was so muddy that the entire tree, roots and all, tumbled backward . . . and right onto my outstretched tail.

It was a large tree, and I couldn't budge it. I was stuck!

Numbat and Silky lifted and pushed, but they could not budge the tree.

Suddenly, the plane door opened and Jenny—and Foosana—ran down the boarding stairs, two steps at a time.

"Look! " Jenny shouted. "The middle of the tree is resting on a rock. If we put all of our weight on the end with the roots, the log will lift right off his tail, like a heavy teeter-totter!"

Everyone raced to the end of the tree and jumped onto the roots. The section of trunk on my tail only lifted an inch or two, but it was enough for me to free my flattened tail, and for the others to swing the fallen ficus away from the plane.

I followed Jenny up the stairs as the others cleared the final twenty yards to the clearing.

Numbat popped back into the pilot seat and began flipping switches and shouting instructions.

I looked at Jenny. Before I could speak, she anticipated my question.

"While you were on your recon mission, Foosana and Lava came to the plane. Lava had already climbed a tree to investigate, and he told us what was happening. We decided our only chance was to fly, so we gassed up the plane and started moving it to the clearing. We figured we'd see you on the way. We didn't have time to wait."

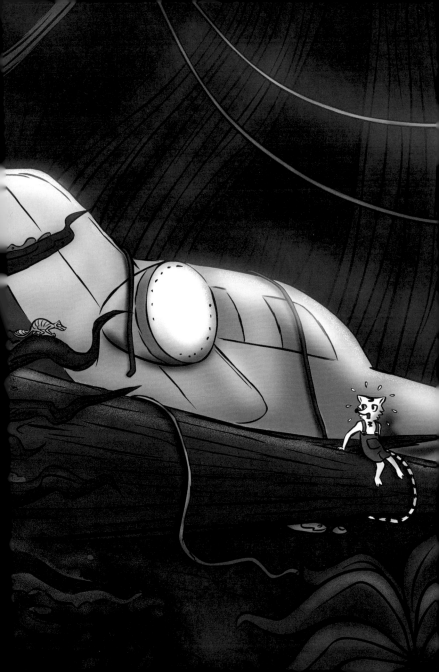

Numbat increased the power, and the plane began to taxi for takeoff. It was bumpy, but we were gaining speed. Numbat pushed the engines to full power, and the front wheels lifted off the ground.

That's when we heard the explosion.

Chapter 18: Escape to Cape Town

The explosion was deafening, even over the noise of the plane's twin engines. We lurched forward, but Numbat confidently eased us back to a steady assent. Not bad for someone who had just learned to fly . . . by reading a book.

"That mega-BooM," Numbat called out, "was the extra fuel storage tank back in our construction zone."

Then he paused. "It's pretty huge that we busted out of there when we did!"

Foosana snarled, *"It's a good thing Lava and I were there to warn you. If you'd waited for*

Oliver to return, all of you would have been cooked!"

I opened my mouth to argue but stopped myself. No one spoke for several seconds, but everyone was looking at me. "Hey, thanks for the help with the fallen ficus back there. What were you two doing out here, anyway?"

Foosana turned defensive immediately. *"Well, all of YOU have been sneaking around and acting suspicious, so we decided to investigate. You told us you were flying to the contest on Air Mad, yet you were building your own airplane. Something didn't add up."*

Lava jumped in. "We, um, saw villagers light the, um, field on fire, but we couldn't, um—"

Foosana cut him off. *"The controlled burn had a perimeter all around us. There was no way out."*

Numbat turned his head and yelled to be heard over the noise of the engines. "The timing of the field barbeque actually makes sense. The forecast now says it's going to start raining late tonight, so they probably timed the burn to start before the storm. I'm just not sure why they were burning THERE ..."

Out of the corner of my eye, I saw a flash that looked like Lava smacking Foosana with his tail. It happened too fast to be sure, and I didn't think anything of it until much later.

We bantered back and forth for a few minutes, before Foosana changed the subject.

"When will we be landing?"

Numbat didn't speak for several more seconds. Then he turned to face us. "So, uh, yea, dudes. Here's the thing. I haven't quite knocked through the WHOLE flight manual yet. There are a lot of words in there, and, you know, I thought we weren't flying until Friday. And— um—landing is, like, in the back of the book. You know?"

"AAGGGGGHHHHHHH! AAGGGGGHHHHHHH!"

Chapter 19: Sunset

Since we couldn't land, we decided to keep flying.

Jenny sat in the co-pilot's seat and charted a course for Cape Town. I sat behind Numbat, reading the flight manual aloud. There were seventy-five very dense and very technical pages about landing. It became clear quite quickly that we were not going to read AND understand all of them before we needed to actually land. We had enough fuel to make it there, but not enough to circle for hours while Numbat learned how to land.

That said, there was no good alternative but to keep trying.

Two hours into the flight, I had to take a break. My mouth was parched from reading the manual aloud, and I was getting hungry. We were flying west, and by this time, we were over the Mozambique Channel. A beautiful sunset filled the windows in front of us. The clouds were a vibrant orange, and flakes of golden sunlight danced on the water below.

The juxtaposition of the beautiful sunset and our dire situation overwhelmed me, and I almost started crying.

Soon the sun was gone below the horizon, and the blackness of the sky matched the bleakness of our situation. I remember thinking, "We can't possibly get out of this one."

I reached in my backpack and pulled out the notes from Tambo. The only light in the cabin was from the dashboard, so I squeezed into the front of the plane to read by its light.

"These notes are to remind you of things you already know. The most important thing to know is that you can do anything. Remember the quote from Henry Ford, 'Whether you think you can, or you think you can't—you're right.'"

Juxtaposition: Placing two things close together to show their differences

These notes are to remind you of things you already know. The most important thing to know is that you can do anything. Remember the quote from Henry Ford, "Whether you think you can, or you think you can't — you're right." - Tambo

Nobody felt like turning on the Christmas lights or the disco ball, so we sat in silence in the dark cabin . . . until we heard an unusual noise coming from under the ratty couch.

Chapter 20: Unusual

It was an unusual noise, but it was not unfamiliar. Even so, Silky slowly backed away from the couch and its noise, clutching his machete.

By the light of the control panel, we saw two hands, then two hairy arms, stretch upward from behind the couch. Then a hairy face with wide, confused eyes squeezed up from between the couch and the airplane's wall.

Captain Aye-Aye was even more surprised than we were.

Chapter 21: Come in, Cape Town

Aye-aye lemurs are nocturnal, and the setting sun had caused Captain Aye-Aye to stir. Apparently he had spent the last few nights at the construction site watching for trouble, looking for clues, and searching for grubs. Instead of going home to sleep for the day, he decided to burrow into the back of one of our couches. At that moment I didn't even care that he had ripped stuffing out of our couch to make a nest. I was just thrilled that he was there.

Captain Aye-Aye was a pilot in the air force before joining the Nature Police, and unlike Numbat, his flight training had included landing.

The mood on the plane changed instantly. Jenny clicked on the Christmas lights, Silky fired up the disco ball, and

---

Nocturnal: An animal that is most active at night is said to be nocturnal.

Numbat, relieved of his pilot duties, jumped on the mechanical bull in the back of the plane. Captain Aye-Aye humored him by banking the plane left and right and up and down to give him quite a rocking ride . . . until he went flying off into the wall. Fortunately, numbats have thick hides.

Only Foosana didn't partake. She curled up on one of the couches, trying to sleep.

After a few hours of revelry, Captain Aye-Aye signaled for me to turn down the music.

"I CAN SEE THE CITY LIGHTS AHEAD. WHICH AIRPORT ARE WE SCHEDULED INTO?"

Numbat stared at him blankly. "We didn't even know we would be landing!"

Captain Aye-Aye picked up the two-way radio. **"CAPE TOWN TOWER, THIS IS *THE SCREAMING LEMUR*. COME IN CAPE TOWN . . . DO YOU COPY?"**

Silence.

"Uh, yeah. I hadn't got to fixing that yet either."

"OK, CREW. HERE IS THE SITUATION, AS FAR AS I CAN TELL. WE CAN'T JUST LAND AT AN AIRPORT WITHOUT HAVING A FLIGHT PLAN ON FILE AND TALKING TO THE CONTROL TOWER. SO WE'RE GOING TO HAVE TO LAND SOMEPLACE OTHER THAN AN AIRPORT . . . WHICH CAN BE PRETTY DICEY. . ."

MisterLemur.com/CT67

- Watch a video of Numbat riding the mechanical bull in flight

Chapter 22: Let's Table This

We'd left in such a hurry that we didn't have any detailed maps. None of us had been to Cape Town. We'd be landing in the dark, and Cape Town is a hilly, rocky city.

We sat in silence for a few more minutes. What a yo-yo of a day. We'd already been back and forth between thinking we might be "done for" and thinking we were going to be fine three different times. Our nerves were shot.

How did we get into this mess in the first place? Was winning some contest, tickling our fancies, and becoming famous really worth it? I thought back to the competition in Tana, and how many bad things we'd avoided by the skin of our teeth to be here. Maybe the universe had been telling us all along that we shouldn't be doing this.

I thought about the feeling of performing "I Brought My Dog to Field Day" and seeing the judges crack up. I thought about the elated feeling as we finished writing "Bad Bean Defect" before the finals.

Then it hit me. When we'd finished writing "Bad Bean Defect," I'd happily pictured our team visiting Table Mountain before the All Africa round. Table Mountain is a famous flat-topped mountain that overlooks the city of Cape Town.

"Let's land on TOP of Table Mountain!" I cried.

Captain Aye-Aye looked at me, contorted his face, and blinked twice. **"UM, PILOTS TRY TO STAY AS FAR AWAY FROM MOUNTAINS AS POSSIBLE."**

"But it's huge! And flat! It's probably the flattest hard surface anywhere near town. Plus, no one lives there, so we don't have to worry about hitting houses or power lines or . . . or . . . anything else!"

Since no one had a better idea, we decided to give it a shot . . . in the dark.

Chapter 23: Penguins

There was almost no light on top of Table Mountain, which was just how Captain Aye-Aye liked it. He sees in the dark as well as people see in the day, and he found the landing conditions to be ideal. The approach and touchdown were surprisingly uneventful.

"Power Clap for Captain Aye-Aye on three! One. . . Two. . . Three!"

CLAP!

We didn't have a hotel reservation, so we slept on the plane. It was cold that night, but it worked. This arrangement suited everyone just fine . . . except Foosana. She had a beautiful dorm room starting Thursday night. So despite the fact that we had just saved her life (or maybe she had helped save ours . . . I wasn't completely sure), she seemed annoyed to be with us.

The next morning, we got word to our families that we were ok, and then Numbat, Silky, Captain Aye-Aye, Jenny, and I spent Wednesday, Thursday, and Friday exploring Cape Town. Foosana and Lava went off on their own, presumably in search of some nicer accommodations.

The rest of us visited the prison-turned-museum on Robben Island, shopped for arts, crafts, and instruments in Greenmarket Square, and posed for pictures with penguins at Boulder's Beach. Cape Town is a very cool town with a lot of history.

Kuils River

Stellenbosch

Strand

Bay

Rooi-Els

Chapter 24: Cape Flats

While our days leading up to the contest were filled with food, walking tours, and sightseeing, Foosana was already working on winning the contest. Her way.

After dinner on Thursday night, Foosana and Lava took the bus to Cape Flats, a particularly dodgy neighborhood on the outskirts of town. This collection of "homemade" corrugated tin houses with no plumbing and intermittent electricity was home to many who were desperate for money and open to unconventional ways of making it. The crime rate was high, and life expectancy was low.

Foosana knew it was just the place to find the person she needed.

Dodgy: dangerous, unreliable, and/or of poor quality

"I'm looking for a . . ." Foosana paused. *"A mechanic."*

It was a slang term she had heard in the movies for someone who "solves problems." The Scheming Lemurs were a problem she wanted solved. And though she wouldn't say it aloud, she had lost confidence in Lava to get it done.

A gap-tooth, dreadlocked man gave her a subtle nod. His eyes darted side to side.

"Be on the corner—by the trench and the barbershop—in ten minutes. Someone will meet you there. Have cash."

The meeting corner had no street light, and Foosana almost missed seeing the man there, leaning against a concrete wall. Lava had become distracted by a small broken mirror and had wandered into the bushes to investigate.

"The Mechanic" whistled softly and waved her over. He wore a hooded sweatshirt, and she couldn't see his eyes. He didn't introduce himself.

"You need something; yes?"

This was new territory for Foosana, and she was nervous. *"There is this competition . . . one team there has become a particular problem. I need to make sure that team does not win. I can give you photos . . ."* her voice trailed off.

"Ƴou wα∩t thꟾм . . . you ᴋ∩ow?" The Mechanic whispered, making a slashing motion across his throat.

"No!" Foosana yelped, more loudly than she intended. The sound pierced the silent darkness, and the man took a step backward.

"I mean—just . . . just be sure they don't win." She swallowed hard. *"Can I count on you?"* Foosana was trying to talk tough, but her knees were shaking.

The Mechanic asked her a few more questions, they talked price, and then she handed him a lunch bag full of money. He counted it quickly, squinting in the darkness. He whispered to himself as he recounted the South African Rand bills, then recounted them again.

"This is only about half the—"

Foosana cut him off. *"I'll bring the rest to this corner Sunday night at 11 p.m., assuming you complete the job."*

His dark eyes studied her. She continued. *"This is all I have with me now. I'm good for the rest."*

The Mechanic squinted again and locked eyes with Foosana, startling her. "Total amateur" he thought, adding "She'll be too scared to try to stiff me." Out loud he agreed, "So 11 p.m. Sunday night. Right here."

Rand: South African money (their "dollar") is called the rand.

Chapter 25: The University of Cape Town

Jenny awoke Saturday morning with a slight cold. We'd been sleeping in the plane for four nights, and, even with the blankets we'd purchased in Greenmarket Square, the mountaintop nights left us all chilled.

We rode the My Citi bus from the base of Table Mountain to the University of Cape Town (UCT), arriving an hour before the 9:00 a.m. start of the contest. The campus was already buzzing. We saw flags from North African countries Morocco and Tunisia, passed a group wearing Ghana T-shirts, and checked in right behind the team from Sierra Leone. We saw a group of tall, lean men in traditional Massai attire, and a group from Egypt wearing a traditional Muslim veil called the hijab.

A local man was selling herbal tea, which he claimed was good for your inner warmth and core. Numbat purchased a paper cup full for Jenny, but the tea was so hot, and the paper cup so flimsy, that the bottom of the cup melted, and the tea spilled all over Numbat's boots before he could deliver her drink.

The upper campus of UCT, where the contest was being held, is situated on the Rhodes Estate on the slopes of Devil's Peak, which is connected to Table Mountain. It actually allowed a reasonably easy commute to campus from the plane. The Rhodes Estate is the former home of businessman Cecil John Rhodes, the founder of the prestigious "Rhodes Scholar" scholarships . . . which would be another really cool thing to win.

Two large dormitories housed many of the competitors, and one of them was Fuller Hall, where Foosana and her team were staying. The contest itself was taking place in

Prestigious: inspiring respect and admiration; having high status

The Jameson Center, a beautiful building where the university hosts graduation and many other events. As we stood outside The Jameson Center admiring its architecture, a teenager approached us.

"My friends, I overhear that you are looking for medicine for the cold?" He smiled broadly. "I am a volunteer with your Competition in Rhyme competition. You may tell me what you need, and I bring for you."

We told him we wanted cold medicine, and he took off jogging.

A female volunteer appeared in the doorway to The Jameson Center. "All contestants: please report to the sign-in table."

"Don't worry, dudes. They won't start for a bit," Numbat reassured us.

We shuffled our feet nervously, waiting for the first volunteer to reappear with medicine. About two minutes passed before the female volunteer appeared again. "Last call!"

she yelled. She kicked the doorstop from under the door and began to close it.

"Wait!" I screamed. "We're coming!"

We all started running toward the door. She saw us and stopped closing it. As we ran, the teenage volunteer caught up to us. "Here! Here is the medicine! I have opened it for you." Jenny grabbed the odd little dark glass bottle from the young man as if they were passing a baton in a relay race. She thanked him without breaking stride, and we made it into the lobby just as the heavy doors closed behind us.

"We don't allow food or liquid inside the briefing room," the door attendant snapped. With that she took our snacks, water bottles, and Jenny's still-unused medicine. "You can get it back after the presentation."

The lead judge for the contest was a large, elegant woman named Jaha. We later learned that Jaha is a Zulu name that means "love." Judge Jaha wore a long, purple robe and traditional Zulu garb. She welcomed us, and, in heavily accented English, explained the rules. Then she repeated them in French, Swahili, and what sounded like Afrikaans. South Africa itself has eleven official languages; I was beginning to see that there were a lot of logistics to presiding over an All Africa finals.

"You will receive a topic and have one hour to prepare a poem or rhyming story, as well as a presentation, for the panel of judges. You can't reuse a subject. Each judge will award each team up to ten points. We give points for entertainment value, wit, rhyme scheme, and presentation. The average score given by the judges is the team's score."

Seventy-two teams were signed up to participate. Of those, the top twenty would advance to the next day's finals. The top four at the end of that day's round would advance to the Hemisphere Finals for the Rivals in Rhyme competition in Sydney, Australia.

Judge Jaha fielded a few questions from the captains, repeating each question and answer in several languages. Our "workshop" space was a series of classrooms in the main building.

Finally, it was time to begin. Judge Jaha pulled a folded piece of paper from the front inside pocket of her robe and announced,

"Your topic for round one of the All Africa finals is . . ."

Chapter 26: Your Futures

"Dude!" Numbat exclaimed. "I, like, just learned all about futures last week. So, these futures things are investments—like stocks or bonds—so you can make money when the price of a crop goes up and down. They're pretty rad. I looked into them after the whole Prince Dude thing went bad. This will be sweet! We can totally rhyme *fluctuation* and *precipitation* in our—"

"That's awesome that you learned that," Jenny interjected, "but I don't think that's what they mean when they say the topic for the finals is "Your Futures."

"Yeah, I think they mean, what will our lives be like in the future? What do you think you will be, you know, when it's 2043?"

That last part just came out like that. I really do think in rhyme . . . at least, most of the time.

Though Numbat was still a little skeptical, we decided to create a song using my idea. We called it *2043*.

In the interest of time, I won't describe the whole process of writing this song, but it went like this: Brainstorm, organize, write, write, write, write, draft, re-write again! Edit, revise (don't forget to capitalize!) write, write, and finally publish at the end.

2043
  By Mister Lemur

What do you think that you will be
when it's two thousand forty-three?

If I were asked to make a bet
I'd say it's not invented yet,
that you'll do something not yet known,
like fix a "Woosh" or fly a "Kone."

Perhaps you'll cure a new disease
or sail a new-found planet's seas
aboard a ship that floats on air
while sitting in the captain's chair.

You have no plan? No need to fret;
your job's not been invented yet!

We all agreed that the future was going to be full of robots, so we created a very industrial, electronic beat and had Jenny sing the song through a microphone with heavy voice effects to simulate a robot voice.

Chapter 27: 2043

With so many contestants, it took nearly three hours to complete all the presentations. To prevent teams from continuing to work on their presentations after the sixty-minute work time was complete, we all had to sit silently in a large room until it was our turn. It was simultaneously boring and nerve-racking . . . and we didn't get to be in the crowd to see any of the other presentations. Captain Aye-Aye, however, was strategically stationed in the audience so he could tell us about the other competitors, and what seemed to tickle the judges' fancies.

The judges loved *2043*, and the crowd "robot danced" like crazy. Jenny's voice started to get hoarse near the end of the song. In retrospect, it might not have been such a good idea to have the lead vocalist on the song be the person with a cold. But we could worry about that later. The Scheming Lemurs put on a great show, and as soon as we walked off stage, we gave ourselves a giant Power Clap.

MisterLemur.com/CT89

- Hear The Scheming Lemurs perform *2043*

Unlike the Madagascar round of the contest, when they announced fourth place, then third, then second, and finally first, the judges here announced first, then second, and so on. All the contestants were invited back into the auditorium to sit in the audience and watch the announcement of the winners.

"Your first-place finisher in the first round is . . ."

A South African a capella group finished first.

The second-place team featured Ethiopian pop star Selam Alem, who did a song called "Hopelessable."

"In third place, from Ranomafana, Madagascar . . ."

"The Scheming Lemurs!"

We gave each other confident nods and fist bumps.

There were twenty teams advancing, so Judge Jaha read through the names quickly. Many of the advancing teams chanted chants or sang patriotic national songs when their names were called. But Judge Jaha just charged forward, turning up her microphone to be heard over the noise.

After Judge Jaha recognized the fifteenth place team, Silky leaned over to me. "Wait—they still haven't called Miss Foosa yet. Have they?"

I wrinkled my nose and shook my head, "No." I craned my neck looking for Foosana and her team in the audience but did not see them. (And doing that made me realize that my neck was still a little sore from the plane crash with The Baron.)

Eighteenth and nineteenth place came and went with no Miss Foosa.

"And in twentieth place, we have a tie for the final spot, so both teams will be advancing. Congratulations to all of our contestants. The final two teams that will advance to the second stage of this weekend's contest are . . . Mount Silly Manjaro from Arusha, Tanzania, and . . . The Kings of Sierra Leone, from Kenema, Sierra Leone."

We looked at each other with eyes wide. "What happened?" "Whoa!" "Dude!"

"We ask that the final twenty—now twenty-one—teams meet back in this room at 16:30, or 4:30 p.m., tomorrow. Please do not be late."

Chapter 29: Silent

We gathered in the lobby of the theater, and Silky, Numbat, and I all began chattering at once, talking over each other, while Jenny finally took her cold medicine.

"The problem with not seeing the other presentations is that we don't know what the judges liked and what they didn't like."

"I'd say they don't like people named Foosana."

"They liked 2043, but what's not to like about that?"

We all talked over each other. Only Jenny was silent. She was slumped quietly in a chair, holding her stomach with her eyes closed.

"I think I've got the flu, or maybe I ate something bad. My stomach feels awful. I really need to lie down."

By the time Captain Aye-Aye had made his way from his seat in the mezzanine level to the lobby, we'd already alerted Judge Jaha about Jenny's condition, and she had called for a doctor. The doctor told us that it appeared quite serious and advised that Jenny drink lots of fluids and spend the next two days in bed. The contest organizers then loaned us a golf cart, and Captain Aye-Aye took Jenny back to the plane to sleep.

Chapter 30: The Campus Coffee Corner

"Dude!" Numbat exclaimed. "I'm so hungry I could eat an anthill. Let's grab grub."

We traipsed over to The Campus Coffee Corner. Numbat and Silky placed our orders, while I headed to the back room to find a quiet table. The room was mostly dark, and it was empty—except for one other table.

"Whoa!" I whispered, doing a double take at the one occupied table. There sat Foosana, sobbing, with her head buried in her hands. She hadn't seen me, and I was tempted to sneak out. But my curiosity, and perhaps my empathy, wouldn't let me.

"May I sit down?"

I had tried to be subtle, but my question startled her. She looked up at me a moment

Empathy: the ability to understand and share the feelings of another through red eyes, sniffled, and then nodded *"Yes."*

"What happened?"

"We were disqualified. They decided our presentation was . . . was . . . off topic."

When Foosana was finished talking, she looked up. Numbat and Silky were standing in the doorway. Numbat sounded sympathetic. "Want me to tickle you? That always makes me feel better." Silky, however, was not. *"Karma's a bit harsh; isn't it?"*

Foosana burst into tears again and ran outside. I hesitated a moment. No one else chased her, so I did. She had such a head start, though, and was so fast, that I lost her before we were even a block from the coffee shop.

When I returned, Silky and Numbat were standing on their chairs having a heated argument. Silky's eyes were popping out of his head in disbelief. *"Terrible idea. I don't trust her."*

Numbat countered. "She'd be rad! I mean, not as rad as a healthy Jenny, but, you know, rad 'til Jenny's good again ..."

I opened my mouth to break it up but stopped. Having Foosana replace Jenny for the rest of the contest was an interesting idea. I listened for a moment to see what reasons and evidence they offered to support their opinions. Neither one was making a good "O.R.E.O." argument (Opinion, Reasons, Evidence, Opinion), instead, they just yelled the same things over and over, louder and louder.

I finally had to say something. "Before we get all snarly at each other, let's go talk to the judges and see if it's even possible within the rules."

MisterLemur.com/CT97

- Hear the song *O.R.E.O.* performed by the Scheming Lemurs

Chapter 31: Second Chance

We were in luck.

Judge Jaha explained, "You must have at least 75 percent of the original lineup, which for you, The Scheming Lemurs, would mean three of the four original members, and you can add at most one new team member."

Once we were off on our own again, we voted on the idea. With no easy way to get in touch with Jenny, the three of us voted. I hoped Jenny wouldn't be mad. I wrote "Yes" on a scrap of paper and put it into Numbat's hat. Silky and Numbat each added a vote as well, and the final tally was two to one in favor of adding Foosana.

She was in her dorm room packing to go home when we approached. I wasn't sure how she'd react, but she was ecstatic, and she responded, *"Yes!"* right away.

Silky, Numbat, and I were halfway down the dorm hall to the stairs when we heard a door slam. I looked up to see Foosana bounding down the hall behind us.

"Wait! Are you still staying in the plane?"

"Uh, yeah. We didn't magically make any money in the last forty-eight hours," **Silky snarked.**

Foosana ignored him and addressed me. *"That's too danger—er—too cold. You might ALL get sick. Come stay in my teammates' room tonight. I'll kick them out. They don't need to be here anymore . . ."*

She did have a point, and we agreed. "We'll ask Captain Aye-Aye to bring our things," I responded.

"Don't tell anyone you are here though. Uh, I . . . I'll have to sneak you in. It's a . . . uh . . . a Fuller Hall security thing."

Ecstatic: Very excited, overjoyed

Foosana

Chapter 32: Good News; Bad News

When Foosana returned, Lava was sitting on the wall waiting for her.

"That's great!" he chirped. "We're, uh, back in!"

Foosana did not share his enthusiasm, and she responded curtly. *"It's not WE; it's ME. And it's great . . . but it's also not great. Don't forget that we just paid someone a lot of money to make sure The Scheming Lemurs lose."*

The little gecko stared back at her, mouth agape.

"We've got to stop The Mechanic without The Scheming Lemurs ever knowing The Mechanic exists . . . and without getting ourselves killed by The Mechanic in the process. I'm going to need your help."

Chapter 33: Selam

After we had brought our things into Fuller Hall, I decided to explore the place. I'd never been in a college dorm, and it seemed fascinating to be in a building where hundreds of college students studied, ate, did laundry, played games, and otherwise lived . . . all under one roof.

As I approached the east stairs, I recognized one of the other contestants struggling to carry two big instrument cases up the stairs.

"May I help?"

She handed me one of the cases, and it took all my strength to carry it up the stairs to the second floor.

When we reached the top, she smiled, and in heavily accented English stated, "Thank you so very much. I am called Selam Alem."

"I'm Oliver, and, hey, congratulations. You are the team that finished second this morning, right?"

"Yes, it was a very big surprise for us." Her shoulders sank. "My songs—they are very popular in my capital city of Addis, but outside of Ethiopia, most people do not stop to listen to them."

I must have looked surprised, because she stopped and sighed. "I'm sorry. I have shared too much."

I smiled what I hoped was a soft and understanding smile. "I can relate. Please, go on." I gestured with my hand for her to continue talking.

"My last name, Alem, means 'world' in my native

language of Amharic, and I would like to be the biggest pop star in the world. We won first place in the Ethiopia contest without much trouble. But if we make it to the next round, I can't imagine people in Australia will be open to hearing our songs."

Ethiopia

Madagascar

Cape Town

"Selam, I didn't get to see your presentation, but there are many talented teams here. If the judges picked you as second, you must be exceptionally talented. I would say that all of us here have things to prove. We've all had setbacks, and we all have self-doubt. If you believe in yourself, you can do anything. Every time you start to say 'I can't do this, or I can't do that,' stop yourself and replace the word can't with the word can. I think you will find that it will change your life. You can do anything that you think you can do . . . if you set a goal and work for it."

We had a late dinner in the UCT dining hall that night, and it was dark when Silky, Foosana, and I walked back to Fuller Hall together. We walked distractedly as we talked, and we ended up lost. The campus is beautiful, so I was happy to continue strolling. We walked past the rugby field and found it unlocked.

"Hey, let's go check it out!"

Foosana seemed hesitant at first, but by the time we reached the center of the field, she was lost in the stars above. She sat down in the middle of the field and smiled.

"What a beautiful view of the Southern Cross. It's amazing to think that you can see this constellation only in the Southern Hemisphere, and that people in the Northern Hemisphere have never seen it . . . unless they have traveled.

"When I was younger, I wanted to be an astronaut. I used to love camping with my parents or finding a quiet place in the park. I'd imagine lines connecting the stars and find the Zodiac's signs. What I really loved was making up my own designs in the stars."

We all looked at the stars, imagining. It was silent for several minutes. My mind drifted to one of my most favorite short poems, and I began speaking it aloud.

Moon View
  By Mister Lemur

I dreamed I woke up on the moon.
I can't remember why.
I noticed when you're on the moon,
the moon's not in the sky.

It was peaceful looking back at earth,
glowing blue, and green, and bright.
It's beautiful here on the moon.
The earth is full tonight.

When I finished, Foosana nodded her head quietly and looked back at the stars. Her face was in a half smile and she looked as if she was fighting back tears. She finally spoke. *"Did you ever think about being an astronaut?"*

"I don't think my parents would let me go that far from home."

She laughed. *"I would have been a great astronaut. They put a monkey into space, why not a fossa? But I soon found that I was really good at singing. Everyone gave me attention for my music. My parents encouraged my singing, and they didn't think it was realistic for a fossa to become an astronaut."*

It was refreshing to see this softer side of Foosana. Silky gently put his lemur hand on her shoulder. "You'd be a great astronaut. I'm sorry you didn't get a chance to chase your dream."

Foosana smiled uncomfortably. She wasn't used to letting her guard down . . . or to Silky being nice to her. I hoped this kinder, gentler team dynamic would carry over to tomorrow. That got me thinking about tomorrow, which was going to be a huge day. "Speaking of home, I'm going back to the dorm. It's getting cold."

Silky wasn't ready to go home yet.

Foosana hesitated. She looked torn between staying there and going back to the dorm.

Before I could say anything else, Silky asked her another question, and soon they had fallen back into conversation. I ambled back to Fuller Hall.

After I left, they continued their giant cosmic game of connect the dots, like artists trying to fill an impossibly large canvas with horses and rocket ships . . . and mirrors, shopping bags, and bell-bottom pants.

"I always wanted to be popular and really good looking. When I was really little my family was captured by men catching silky sifaka lemurs for a zoo. They took my whole family but turned me loose because they felt I—I . . . I wasn't cute enough. Can you believe it? I bet they'd be amazed to see me now!"

They both laughed out loud, and their laughter echoed off the empty metal bleachers. For the first time, Silky noticed how alone they were in the big empty stadium, and he started to get spooked.

"I think it's time for us to head home, too," he whispered.

Ambled: To walk or move at a slow, relaxed pace

Chapter 35: Duct Tape

Silky and Foosana were tip-toeing nervously out of the stadium when they heard a gruff voice behind them.

"You! Freeze!"

"Oh, no! It's the security—" Silky blurted.

Before he could finish his sentence, a large man grabbed him and immediately put duct tape over his mouth. Silky wriggled for all he was worth, but the grip was too strong. He was freaking out, but no one could hear his muffled cries. Suddenly, the man dropped him, and Silky fell to the ground.

He looked up and saw the man clutching his arm where Foosana had just bitten him with her powerful jaws. She took off running in one direction, and Silky ran in another.

In predictable lemur fashion, Silky ran for the safety of the nearest tree, bounding off the grass toward the trunk. An instant before he reached the tree, two large hands brought a burlap sack down over him. He heard the *thhhh* sound of duct tape being wrapped around the open end of the sack. Silky was thrown roughly into the back of a van. Within moments, they were on the N2 highway heading east toward Cape Flats.

Chapter 36: Sunday Morning

Foosana and Lava were on the bus from UCT to Cape Flats before the sun began to rise. The kidnapping had happened only a few hours before, and between adrenaline and worry, Foosana had hardly slept. This was not the way to start the biggest day—so far—of her life.

As they trudged through Cape Flats' dirt streets, Foosana whispered to Lava, *"This place sure looks different in the daylight. Not so scary, just more . . . depressing."*

Most residents were just starting the day. Many were still wrapped in blankets as they warmed kettles of water over outdoor fire pits. The long rows of squalid dwellings stretched out in front of them for miles, with no street signs and few location markers

Squalid: a place that is extremely dirty and unpleasant, especially as a result of poverty or neglect visible to the untrained eye. Feral dogs roamed the streets in mangy, menacing packs. There was a reason this place was not in most Cape Town tourist guide books.

They walked on for about ten minutes, until Lava, who has no hair himself, noted, "They seem to have an, uh, unusually high number of barbershops."

Foosana froze and looked at Lava with a "Why didn't I think of that?" expression.

Feral dog: a dog that has changed from being domesticated to being wild or untamed

114

"Barbers and hairstylists know everyone in their neighborhoods! They're the town gossips!"

Most of the barbershops were just people's homes—their shacks—with barber signs in front. Even at this early hour, nearly all were "open," but none had any customers.

Foosana hadn't seen enough of The Mechanic's face in the dark Thursday night to describe him, so she asked for him, usually awkwardly, by his profession. Some looked scared by the question, while others just claimed they didn't know the answer. None offered any helpful advice.

After the twelfth consecutive unsuccessful barber stop, Foosana was ready to cry. The Scheming Lemurs had already replaced one original member. If they couldn't get Silky back for the start of the contest, they would be disqualified. Her chance at stardom was dimming quickly, and she knew it was her fault.

Foosana sat down to think, resting against a telephone pole. The harder Foosana tried to think, the fewer ideas that came to her. Soon she was thinking so intently *about* thinking that she wasn't thinking effectively at all.

But she *had* to think. Was there a way to get Captain Aye-Aye's help without alerting him that—

"Um—Foosana—I think you should, um, come over here." Lava gestured to Foosana, who slowly stood. "Over here. By this, uh, telephone pole. This is the same broken, um, mirror that I was looking at, um, looking at when we were here before. This is the same area where, um, The Mechanic lives!"

Chapter 37: Sayonara, Silky?

Jenny was the first to awaken, and the first to see the problem.

"Hey, have you guys seen Silky? It looks like he didn't make it to bed last night . . ." She whispered hoarsely, gesturing toward his neatly made section of the bed.

I raised myself onto my elbows and wrinkled my face in groggy thought. Then I gasped. "He was talking with Foosana on the rugby field last night!"

Jenny knocked on Foosana and Lava's dorm room door, but there was no response. When Captain Aye-Aye got home that morning to go to bed, he shimmied onto the balcony and over to their window. Thick curtains blocked his view, and the sun's glare off the window hurt his light-sensitive eyes.

"THERE IS NOTHING TO REPORT, AS FAR AS I CAN TELL." Then he climbed into his corner of the bed and fell asleep.

Chapter 38: Finders Weepers

 Eventually Foosana did find The Mechanic. But she didn't find him in a good mood.

"You should not have come here asking for me. We can't talk here." He growled, gesturing with his hooded head toward a little shack that looked much like all the other shacks. "Rookies are so high maintenance," he thought.

The Mechanic led her through an open door frame into a sparse, colorless room. Then he lit a candle and dragged open a makeshift iron door into another dark, inner room. There The Mechanic set the candle on the floor. The flickering light danced off the rough, corrugated steel walls. He struck a match and lit two more candles before motioning for her to sit. There were no seats in the room, so Foosana sat on the cold dirt floor.

The Mechanic remained standing. He didn't acknowledge Lava, who was climbing in and out of little holes and wandering distractedly.

Foosana spoke first. *"There's been a change in plans. I need you to let the lemur go. But not until after I leave, so he doesn't know I was—."*

"Did you bring the rest of the money?" he interrupted curtly.

Foosana hadn't brought any money, other than a few Rand for the bus ride home and maybe some breakfast. Even if she'd thought of it, she didn't have the money to bring. She had been counting on either using prize money from the contest to pay what she owed, or just getting out of the country before The Mechanic could find her.

But Foosana was cool. She exhaled the tension from her shoulders and forced a smile.

"I'm bringing it at 11:00 tonight, like we talked about. That's the deal; right?"

The Mechanic did not smile back. "The deal is already in motion. The first lemur is not the only lemur that is going to get it." He paused. "Speaking of 'getting it,' your decision to bite me on the arm last night is going to come back to bite you."

Foosana felt her stomach sink and her temperature rise. She had no idea the man she bit the night before was The Mechanic. She wished she could disappear. Lava practically did. He involuntarily turned the color of the ground beneath him and blended into the darkened corner. There were so many lizards around that The Mechanic hadn't really even noticed Lava.

The Mechanic barked something loudly in Zulu, and two men entered the room. One put a dog muzzle over Foosana's snout while the other blindfolded her. It was too tight and smelled of dog hair. And it was totally humiliating.

Lava took one last look at Foosana and slipped through a rusted-out section of the metal wall and out into the street.

Chapter 39: Theories

Lava was exhausted when he finally made it back to Fuller Hall. He found us sitting on a table in the student lounge, exchanging far-fetched theories about Silky's disappearance. We didn't notice him enter. Lava dragged himself onto the table and began speaking with unusual clarity. The urgency in his voice even woke Captain Aye-Aye, who'd been curled in a ball of warm, fuzzy sleep in the corner.

"Silky and Foosana have been kidnapped. I know where they are. Or, uh, at least, where they were a few hours ago. I need your help to, um, rescue them."

The group sat in silence as Lava spun a story about how the two were both kidnapped the night before, and how he had heroically stowed away in the kidnappers' truck to learn their location. I pulled up a map and then looked at the clock. "We're going to have to hurry," I proclaimed, "and we're going to have to drive."

"I, uh, don't think we should all go. I didn't see many guards, and the location was just a house, well, a, uh, shack. Also, if we all go, we're going to, uh, really stick out as odd there."

"I got us into this mess. I'll go, and I'll take Lava and Captain Aye-Aye. Numbat, you stay behind in case someone needs to rescue the rescuers!"

Chapter 40: Nocturnal by Nature

Forty minutes later, we had parked the car, and Lava, Captain Aye-Aye, and I were walking quietly down a hard-packed dirt street in Cape Flats. The ground was so hard that the gophers stayed away, and the people were harder than the dirt. It wasn't cold, but Captain Aye-Aye shivered anyway.

He wore dark glasses, not so much to be *incognito*—or in disguise—but rather in hopes of fooling his nocturnal nature. He even carried a large cup of coffee in one of his hairy hands. Captain Aye-Aye almost never drank coffee in the morning.

We looped around the shack where Lava had last seen Foosana and approached quietly from the back. Captain Aye-Aye was already on edge, and he didn't need any reminders to be careful.

A family sat in front of the house, talking around a smoldering fire pit.

Lava whispered, "Hmm, uh, you'll get noticed. Wait here. I'll, uh, look around inside."

Being a little lizard in an area full of little lizards has its advantages. Unless he was headed for the kitchen, most adults didn't think twice when they noticed him . . . if they noticed him at all. Leaf Geckos are not indigenous to South Africa, but in Cape Flats, where people, disease, and even snakes were persistent dangers, little lizards rarely warranted a second look.

He had to watch out for kids though. And dogs. Both loved to scoop up lizards and play with them . . . or worse. The kids by this particular fire pit looked both bored enough to chase him and lean, wiry, and quick enough to actually catch him. Lava scurried carefully around the side. He was nervous but also excited. Both Foosana and Mister Lemur would be so proud of him. For the first time in his life, he was about to be a real hero.

Lava climbed in through the same rusted section of wall he'd used as an escape route earlier that morning. It took a moment for his eyes to adjust from the bright sunshine to the darkness inside the shack. When they did, he was amazed at what he saw.

He began to make out a dirt floor, then some bare walls . . . and nothing else. There were no prisoners, no furniture, no clothing, no anything, really, except some pieces of garbage. Lava sighed. Silky and Foosana could be anywhere in Cape Flats.

Chapter 41: Pacing

Back at Fuller Hall, Numbat paced the hallway outside Foosana's room.

Each time his pacing took him by the restrooms, he'd check the clock that hung on the wall there. The clock read 12:30. It was only four hours before the start of the final round. He tried not to think about what might be happening in Cape Flats.

Chapter 42: Nervous Talker

It's probably better that Numbat didn't know what was happening in Cape Flats. It wasn't so much that it was bad. It just wasn't anything good. In reality, it wasn't really anything at all. And precious minutes were ticking away.

Captain Aye-Aye, Lava, and I were back out on the hard-packed streets of Cape Flats, indecisively passing shack after shack. That's when I realized Captain Aye-Aye was a "nervous talker."

"SO THE PLACE WAS COMPLETELY EMPTY, HUH? THEY PROBABLY LEFT BECAUSE THEY EXPECTED A SEARCH PARTY. DID IT LOOK LIKE THEY LEFT IN A HURRY? DO YOU THINK THEY SAW YOU

WHEN YOU FOLLOWED THEM? YOU SEE THAT HOUSE OVER THERE? THAT LOOKS ODD. OF COURSE, EVERY HOUSE HERE LOOKS ODD TO ME. DO YOU KNOW . . . ?"

There must have been ten thousand ramshackle homes and makeshift stores in the township. Maybe more. And although everything looked a little suspicious, nothing looked more suspicious than anything else, and nothing seemed particularly worthy of investigation.

"I WONDER WHERE THE SCRAP METAL USED IN THESE HOMES COMES FROM? I'LL BET THE SOUND OF RAINDROPS ON THE ROOF IS REALLY LOUD WHEN—"

For the first time in what seemed like fifteen minutes, Captain Aye-Aye stopped talking.

There in front of us was a building that looked suspiciously different than the usual mix of homes and shops. The building had a serious-looking gate outside, bars on the building's few windows, and a sturdy metal door. A large and menacing mutt-dog rested on the dirt that would have been the lawn, had any grass been able to grow there. He was missing a large chunk of one ear, and he looked as if he'd been in more fights than Silky had been in boutiques. An even larger man with a sour look on his face leaned against the building wall, a few feet from the door, standing guard. The place even smelled funny.

We quickly ducked into a drainage pipe and out of view.

"That's GOT to be it. We'll have to find a side door or a window."

I peeked out of the pipe, looking for a different entrance. A new man I hadn't seen before was walking toward the guard, carrying a stack of cash in one hand.

"Ransom money!" I whispered. "They must have other prisoners!"

Lava really hoped he didn't end up as a prisoner. He doubted prisoners ate well. He swallowed hard and scurried out of the drain pipe and across the road. When he reached the fence around the building, he noticed a bird was watching him with hungry eyes. Great; just what he needed.

He darted along the base of the fence until he found an area where runoff from the last big rain had eroded the dirt. There was a tiny gap beneath the fence, just big enough to squeeze under. He wriggled through the hole and darted his way to a small window. He looked inside and felt a sinking feeling.

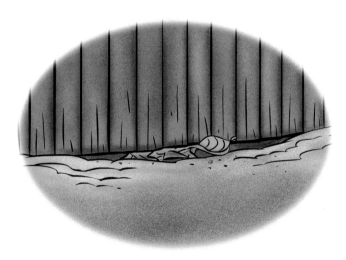

Chapter 43: Bellhop Stop

Numbat and Jenny were sitting in the lobby of Fuller Hall when Jenny's watch chirped 3:00. They made silent eye contact for a moment before Numbat subtly nodded his head to say, "Okay. I'm going." He had loaded their rented instruments onto a borrowed bellman-style dolly, and he began pushing the dolly out the door and across campus to The Jameson Center.

They hadn't heard from the others, but it was time to check in for the finals. Jenny watched through tired, bloodshot eyes as Numbat walked away. Then she turned and staggered back to their room to go to bed.

Numbat had just rounded the first tree-lined turn toward The Jameson Center when a somewhat familiar-looking teenager approached him.

"My friend, your load is so heavy!" the boy
practically sang. "Here, I will help you. I am a
volunteer with your, uh, Rivals in Competition contest."
Without waiting for an answer, he hip-checked
Numbat out of the way and began pushing the
dolly of instruments. Numbat appreciated the
help, as the load was almost unmanageably
large for someone his size. But something
seemed just a little off.

The teen began to walk quickly, and Numbat had to power walk just to keep up. Numbat had stacked the instruments on the cart but not tied them on, and they were beginning to jiggle on the fast-moving cart. His rented guitar looked precariously close to falling onto the hard stone path. Without saying a word, Numbat sprang onto the cart to secure his guitar, in the process knocking my bass guitar case from the stack. It crashed down on the would-be bellhop's head. He staggered momentarily and then collapsed onto the cart, knocked out cold.

No one had witnessed the accident, and there was no one else nearby. So Numbat simply climbed down from the top of the pile and once again took his place at the back of the dolly. With an oomph, he began pushing his load—now both the instruments and the knocked-out boy on top—toward the competition.

Chapter 44: Leftovers

Lava didn't stay on his window perch long. Hungry glances from the birds kept him on the move. But he did stay there long enough to get a good look inside, and that look was very revealing. The large metal door, the barred windows, and the security guard all made sense now. The building was . . . a bank. Just a boring old bank . . . and a dead-end lead.

Captain Aye-Aye and Lava were totally dejected. And hungry. We walked on down the street for another ten minutes until the irresistible smell of banana rice began to waft our way.

"Hey, let's, uh, follow that smell. Maybe they've got some, uh, leftovers."

This was wishful thinking on Lava's part. Food and money were scarce in Cape Flats, and no one let food go to waste on purpose.

We followed our noses to a four-room house. Four rooms is large by Cape Flats' standards, suggesting the family was relatively well-to-do. Maybe they actually would have extra food lying around.

Several men played soccer in the street in front of the house, and a pack of wiry dogs ran about, alternately chasing the ball, the players, and each other.

If the front side of the house resembled a block party, the back resembled a ghost town. We effortlessly scaled the back fence, slipped into the yard, and moved toward the kitchen. We cowered against the fence as a woman walked out of the house, carrying an old soda bottle filled with water. She walked purposefully toward the soccer players, and her peripheral vision didn't pick up the unusual trio of intruders.

When she stepped out through the gate into the street, Captain Aye-Aye whispered, **"THIS IS OUR CHANCE!"**

Lava and Captain Aye-Aye scampered into the now-empty kitchen while I stood watch by the door. We knew they might have only a minute or two before she returned.

A scalding-hot iron pot of banana rice was suspended by a chain above a small wood fire. That chain was stretched tightly between two food-splattered posts, and the center was blackened from years of resting over a flame. Light gray wisps of smoke drifted around the pot and up through a large, crude chimney. The pot had no lid, and a large, hand-carved wooden ladle with an ornate handle extended

from the top.

Captain Aye-Aye looked at Lava. **'IT'S TOO HOT TO EAT NOW. WE'RE GOING TO NEED TO PUT SOME IN A CONTAINER UNTIL IT COOLS.'**

They looked around the room anxiously. There was so little furniture in the room that it took only a few seconds to assemble an inventory. Captain Aye-Aye's eyes settled quickly on a rusty old toolbox on the floor by one wall. The lid was open. Perhaps there was something inside they could use.

They had just reached the toolbox when the dogs began barking excitedly. I chirped like a Myna bird to signal danger. Captain Aye-Aye stiffened and listened. The barking was getting louder, and it was coming his way. I scampered up to the roof, but the others were stranded against a wall in plain sight. The dogs were now just steps from being in the kitchen.

Captain Aye-Aye felt a rush of panic. He sprang into the rusty toolbox and closed the lid. Lava ducked between the toolbox and the wall, and changed color.

Most of the dogs ran to their still-empty bowls, near the fire pit, looking back at the door impatiently. One dog, however, ran directly to the now-closed toolbox, and he began barking excitedly. Soon three other dogs joined him in a frenzy of barks. The deep, angry sounds of the gruff voices reverberated off the inside of the toolbox, amplifying the noise. Captain Aye-Aye felt sick.

He heard footsteps approach the toolbox and then a man's voice yelling at the dogs. Lava recognized The Mechanic right away and panicked. His little lizard legs scurried up the wall as fast as they would go. This, of course, caused the dogs to become even more animated.

The Mechanic shook his head and growled to the dogs mockingly. "Such smart guards. I am protected from little lizards!"

Reverberated: a loud noise repeated several times as an echo

The dogs, and their astute noses, were not discouraged. They continued to bark at the toolbox until The Mechanic began distributing some meager food scraps and a few dry kibbles into their bowls. The woman lifted the hot pot of banana rice and took one step toward the door before The Mechanic stopped her.

"Leave some food for the hostages. Not too much, but we want to keep them alive. We are more likely to get paid that way."

Chapter 45: Involuntary

When he arrived at the contest to check in, Numbat alerted the other staff of the injured volunteer. He was a little nervous that The Scheming Lemurs would be disqualified for knocking out a staff member . . . even if it was an accident.

He quickly realized he had bigger things to worry about.

"That's not one of our volunteers," the woman at the front desk informed him. "All of our volunteers are wearing nametags . . . and I've never seen this man in my life."

An ambulance was summoned, and the teen was loaded onto a stretcher.

"Do you know this man?" one of the paramedics asked Numbat.

"No, I've never seen . . ." Numbat's voice trailed off. He looked at the man on the stretcher again and a thought began to bubble up in his mind. "Wait. Yes. Yes! I have. This is the volunteer who helped me get cold medicine for Jenny yesterday. He seemed like he was, I mean, I hope he still is, a very cool dude."

The event organizers looked at Numbat skeptically. They put their heads together in a huddle and whispered for a few moments. Judge Jaha emerged looking concerned and announced definitively,

"No, this is most definitely not one of our volunteers."

Chapter 46: The Reverse Santa Claus

The Mechanic dished two small bowls of banana rice and set them aside. The dogs finished eating the scraps in seconds and then resumed barking at the toolbox. The largest of the dogs even pushed the box with his nose, causing it to fall back into the wall. Fortunately, the lid stayed closed.

The Mechanic yelled a few words at the dogs in a language I couldn't understand, and then took them outside, where he chained them in the front yard. As soon as the pack was outside, the woman reached down for the toolbox. She pulled it away from the wall, locked it, and carried it to the kitchen counter where she was putting things away. "Honestly. What does he keep in here?"

Lava found me lying flat on the flat roof, and he gave me the update. With Captain Aye-Aye in the toolbox, The Mechanic had three hostages, but was only aware of two. "Lava, you can move more freely inside. Go look around and see where Silky and Foosana are and report back to me."

The house was small enough that it didn't take long for Lava to find Foosana and Silky. There was no formal lock on the door, just a piece of wood stuck through the door handle to keep it from opening. Thank goodness for simple construction.

"Okay, what is happening out the back door?" I whispered.

"Too crowded."

"The front?"

"Big dogs."

"Hmm. Scamper across the roof and see if the house has a side window. And be careful not to fall in the chimney vent."

As soon as I whispered "chimney vent," it hit me. In houses like these, the chimneys are not for fireplaces, but to vent smoke from the wood-burning cooking stove . . . which is always in the kitchen . . . which is where Captain Aye-Aye was locked in the toolbox.

"Okay, Lava, I have a plan. If you can create a distraction to get the woman out of the room, I can free the others. We'll meet back at the car. We can all scamper up the chimney and onto the roof, then get to the neighbor's house without . . ." My voice trailed off as I thought about what I was saying. "Go look at the vent and see if we can actually climb that."

Lava reported back that the vent was too tall, steep, and smooth to free climb . . . even for a lemur. We sat in deflated silence for a long moment. Finally, another thought came to me: "Lava, I want you to look around everywhere, and see if you can find any rope or chain or heavy wire."

Lava had been gone only a couple of minutes, when I started thinking about how long this operation was taking. The odds of us getting back to UCT in time for the final round were growing longer every moment.

"A rope and, um, chain is being used to tie up the dogs. The guards are, uh, playing soccer in front of the building, and they've used another rope to, um, make goals."

"Are they playing in shoes or barefooted?"

"Uh, barefooted, I think. At least, um, some of them. Why?"

"Okay, Lava. Here's what I need you to do. I need you to pull the shoelaces out of as many pairs of shoes as you can without getting caught."

His mouth hung open in disbelief.

I continued. "Not the shoes they are wearing. The shoes of the people who are barefooted. And I need you to do it quickly. Then bring them back here."

Lava brought back six shoelaces, and I tied them together into a rope. It wasn't very strong, but lemurs aren't very heavy.

"Umm, what are you, uh, going to do?"

"The Reverse Santa Claus. We will go up the chimney."

The roof was flat and made up of a few pieces of corrugated steel wedged together. I found a seam between pieces and anchored one end of the shoelace rope to that seam. Then we dangled the other end down the chimney, but not so far that they could see it in the kitchen.

Lava again snuck into the kitchen, grabbing a spoon and a small metal bowl. He crept quietly to the front door and then began running around the front yard on his two hind legs. He loudly banged the spoon on the bowl and began impersonating a fire engine. He sounded like a baboon celebrating New Year's Eve, and he got EVERYONE's attention.

I was using every muscle in my face trying not to laugh as I slid down the chimney and ran to the room where Foosana and Silky were held. After removing the stick that held their door closed, I sprinted back to the kitchen and found the locked toolbox. I pulled on the rusty latch but it wouldn't open. I pushed up, then pulled down, then—in desperation—tried to take the whole thing. It was heavier than expected, and toppled off the table.

Ka-CLANK!

YAAAAAAAAHHHH!

The lock on the rusty toolbox finally surrendered when it crashed to the ground, scattering screwdrivers, wrenches, and one startled aye-aye lemur onto the hard dirt floor.

"ARE YOU TRYING TO RESCUE ME OR KILL ME?" Captain Aye-Aye yelped.

He didn't have much time to be ungrateful before the sound of the toolbox alerted The Mechanic. Soon the familiar sound of clinking collars, guttural growls, and claws on clay was upon us. Foosana and I grabbed Captain Aye-Aye and began to follow Silky up the makeshift rope. Lemurs are excellent climbers, and Captain Aye-Aye, even in his slightly dazed state, was on the roof in about three seconds.

I had just started up the ladder when The Mechanic and his soccer-playing friends came running into the kitchen. They looked furious. They were half way across the room, covering ground in long, athletic strides, when one of the players slipped on the spilled tools. That player fell into The Mechanic, who then fell into another player, as all three tumbled into the pack of frenzied dogs.

By the time they were back on their feet, I had reached the top of the chimney, and

Foosana was starting her climb. That's when the shoelace-rope began to break. She was the heaviest of the group, and probably the weakest climber. I looked down. She didn't say a word, but her eyes screamed "Help!" I did the only thing I could think of.

"Climb my tail!" I dropped my long, ringed tail down the chimney for her to climb like a rope.

A ring-tailed lemur's tail is longer than his body. Normally a lemur with a fossa holding onto his tail is in big trouble. The pursuit of fame can lead to some odd situations.

I felt a strong pull on my tail and nearly fell over. For a moment I thought we were both going to be pulled back down the chimney to the waiting pack of dogs below.

I looked down to see The Mechanic holding my tail tightly in one of his strong hands. He hissed, "I was going to let them go tomorrow if they had just stayed put. Now, I'm going to make you all into chew toys for my dogs."

In a flash, Foosana slid back down my tail, bit The Mechanic's hand, and scampered up my tail. The Mechanic let go, and we sprinted across the rusty roof, bounding from one neighbor's shack to the next until the angry voices and barking dogs faded into the distance behind us.

We didn't stop running until the car was running, and soon we were screeching away from Cape Flats.

I gasped. "Did you hear that?!?"

Foosana hesitated. *"Hear what?"*

"That man yelled he was going to let you go tomorrow if you just stayed put."

"So?"

"So . . . if he wasn't kidnapping you for ransom, why would he hold you for today and let you go tomorrow?"

"Because . . . he . . ." Silky wrinkled his nose in thought. Then his eyes got big. *"The contest!"*

"You're right. Someone doesn't want US to win this contest. We've got to get back and warn the others."

Chapter 47: Directions

Numbat waited nervously in the gathering room as the clock approached—and then struck—4:30.

Judge Jaha promptly stepped to the podium and began speaking. She introduced the topic for the final round as "directions."

It may have been his imagination, but no one seemed to notice—or at least, to care—that Numbat was the only one sitting at The Scheming Lemurs' table.

Chapter 48: A Plan

The first few minutes of the car ride back had been a rush of conversation. We'd decided to get Silky, Foosana, Lava, and me back to the competition, while Captain Aye-Aye would get Jenny, and move the plane. We didn't know who was in cahoots with The Mechanic, or if he knew where the plane was, but it seemed as if we needed to assume the worst.

Chapter 49: On Topic

When we reached the contest center, there were twenty five minutes left on the clock for work time. The others waited outside while I walked up to the check-in table and told a little fib.

"Hi. I left my workshop room to use the bathroom, and now I can't remember what the room number is."

Silky pressed one of his amazing ears against the door to listen.

"Let's see . . . The Scheming Lemurs. You are in room A-14. You'd better hurry back to your room though, you have only 24 minutes left to prepare your presentation!" With that, I scampered off down "A Hall" while the others snuck around to a back door.

Numbat had to be expecting us, but he still looked startled when we entered, everybody shouting at once.

"What's the topic?"

"Have you written anything?"

"Are you ok?"

Numbat looked glum. "I wrote a directionless story about my friends forgetting the driving directions right before a big contest"

I cut him off. "Directions?"

He nodded, and I ran to the board. "Ok, let's start brainstorming! We could write a song about giving good directions . . ."

"What makes some directions good directions?"

Numbat started, "You know, they are, like, totally clear and super easy to get."

Foosana continued "Okay. What specifically makes them totally clear and easy to... understand?"

Numbat opened his mouth to talk, but nothing came out. I spoke up.

"Well . . . good directions are accurate, for one thing. And . . . and, they have lots of prepositions!"

I looked around the room. Everyone was nodding but avoiding eye contact with me, in that way you do in class when you want to look like you know the answer but really hope you don't get called on to answer a question.

After a few awkward seconds of silence, I bailed them out.

"Prepositions are words or phrases that specify place, time, and direction. Words such as on, beside, in front of, before, after. . . . You can't really give good directions without good prepositions. They're words that tell you where you're going."

The songwriting dynamic with Foosana was a challenge. We were all into the

prepositions idea, but Foosana and I had very different ideas of what to do with it. She had a vision for a pop song called "Preposition Popcorn" with keyboard sound effects simulating prepositions "exploding" like popcorn kernels as she danced through a scavenger hunt. I 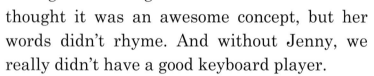 thought it was an awesome concept, but her words didn't rhyme. And without Jenny, we really didn't have a good keyboard player.

Foosana thought my song was boring, and we began to argue. She tore up the page of lyrics I'd written. I could never imagine Jenny doing that. I wished she were here instead of Foosana.

In the heat of the moment, we lost track of time, but we must have been back and forth for nearly five minutes. Five very valuable minutes. We might still be arguing if Numbat hadn't interrupted us.

Above the sound of the argument, Numbat shouted, "Boom-Shaka-Laka!"

"Oh My!" We all responded in unison. That is our call to get everyone's attention in a noisy room.

"So, dudes!" (Numbat calls everyone "Dude.") "While you two were in your bark-fest, I took your notes and whipped up this little ditty. I call it "Preposition Punk." It's a duet for me and Foosana."

We liked it and set to learning it as fast as possible. The guitar part was fairly simple, and since it was a duet, Numbat and Foosana got to split up memorizing the lyrics.

With four minutes left on the clock, we were still busy working. Suddenly, I heard the door open. Foosana gasped and then slammed the door shut and locked it. We all stopped playing and looked up.

"We can't go out that way. The Mechanic and two of his friends are in the hallway."

Numbat looked confused. "The what?" We hadn't had time to explain the situation to Numbat.

I looked around the room, just as I heard someone start to jiggle a key—or a screwdriver—or something—in the lock.

I yelped. "The air ducts! It always works in the movies. Let's go!"

If there was one advantage to Jenny's absence, it was that everyone else was a small and nimble critter . . . a lemur, a numbat, a leaf gecko, or a fossa. In no time at all, we were scampering into, through—and then out of—the air conditioning ducts above the ceiling. We emerged into a restroom right next to the judges' chambers.

We popped out of the restroom into an area full of legitimate volunteers. We'd be safe here. But after the contest, it would likely be a different story.

Because we were submitting our rhyme right at the one-hour deadline, we were caught in a big rush of others doing the same. I could only keep Judge Jaha's attention for a moment.

"Could you call the police, please, Judge? There are three men here who are trying to keep us from winning the contest."

I guess I didn't say it very convincingly because Judge Jaha just laughed. "You certainly do have an active imagination, young man!"

I didn't know this until later, but Judge Jaha had already called the police. She'd been troubled by the appearance of the fake volunteer and didn't want to take any chances. She wasn't going to interrupt the proceedings, of course, but had decided to invite a pair of policemen to sit in the audience . . . just in case.

Chapter 50: Preposition Punk

And then, in a whirl, it was time for The Scheming Lemurs to hit the stage. Holding our breaths that it would all come together, we did an exuberant rendition of "Preposition Punk."

MisterLemur.com/CT164

- See the awesome video of Numbat, Foosana, Silky, and me performing *Preposition Punk*

Chapter 51: Grave Danger

We'd just finished exchanging high-fives backstage after our presentation. As I was coming down from the performance excitement, Selam Alem appeared at my shoulder.

"May I talk with you a moment?" she whispered. She gestured toward a quiet corner. I nodded silently and followed her. "I think you and your friends are in a most grave danger." She looked around quickly, then continued whispering in her accented, broken English. "Two men, they were talking, in the hall, before you performed. They are to kidnap you at the end. They are bad men. They have many, many men... twenty, maybe more."

Chapter 52: The Envelope, Please

Twenty-one teams started the final round. It quickly became clear that none of them had made it this far without being good. Now the judges were about to announce the four teams—just four teams!—from the entire continent that would advance. Each of the four finalists would get an all-expense paid trip to the next round of the competition in Sydney, Australia. The fifth-place finishers would get . . . to sit on their couch and watch the competition on TV like everyone else.

With such a small number of teams in the finals (compared to the first round) we didn't have to wait long to learn our fate. At least, our fate as it related to the contest.

The sixth-place team was announced first, then the fifth, fourth, and third-place teams. Judge Jaha turned away from the mic and whispered something to one of the other judges.

I closed my eyes and squeezed Jenny's hand. My heart was racing.

Judge Jaha turned back to the crowd and music began to play. And now, ladies and gentlemen, we're going to take a short commercial break. We'll be right back!

"Aahh! This is not good for my heart!" Silky yelped.

The commercial break seemed to drag on for five minutes before Judge Jaha resumed speaking.

"In Second place," the judge announced ". . . the musical styling's of. . . The Scheming Lemurs!"

"In first place, from Addis Ababa, Ethiopia, Ethio-Pop sensation Selam Alem! We'd like to invite Selam and her band on stage to perform their Rivals in Rhyme winning poem-turned-song 'Yes, I Can.' This is an inspirational song with a wonderful message. If you believe in yourself, your heart will give you directions to follow your dreams."

I was really happy for her. I wished it had been us in first place, but unlike the Madagascar round of Rivals in Rhyme, the top four finishers here each received all-expense-paid trips to the next round. So other than bragging rights, being first really wasn't much different than being second. . . or fourth.

Selam and her band took the stage to a thunderous round of applause. The drummer began the beat, and Selam implored the crowd to clap along with her. Soon everyone in the auditorium was standing and clapping.

Well, almost everyone. As Selam surveyed the crowd, she noticed one man near the front who was not clapping. Instead, he was slyly raising a blow dart tube to his lips and aiming it toward Silky in the second row.

"Everybody clapping! That means you, too! You, over there!" Selam shouted, pointing to the man. Instantly, two spotlights shown on the would-be assassin, and about a thousand pairs of eyes looked to see what sort of Scrooge was not dancing to this contagious beat. The man smoothly tucked his blow dart contraption behind his ear as though it were a pencil and he was a reporter.

None of us had looked fast enough to realize what was happening. Selam saw that she had bought us a few minutes but knew we were still in imminent danger. These guys are clever, she thought. A gun would make too much noise, but no one would hear a poison dart in a crowded theater.

"All right, very good!" she exhorted the clapping, swaying crowd. "You all look ALIVE tonight! Let's keep it that way! I want now to invite the other three winning teams onto the stage. We will sing together!"

The crowd roared at this, and she turned and began whispering instructions to her band.

We danced our way onto the stage, and Selam's band members began yelling

---

Exhort: to strongly encourage or urge someone to do something instructions to those who played the same instruments they did. It was so loud that we could barely hear them. They told us the chords to play, as well as a few other instructions.

We "vamped" on the song for a few more moments, and then Selam began singing.

I will dream big dreams
And follow them.
I will always say "I can."
I will never say "I can't."
I will always say "I can."
I will never say "I can't."

She sang the chorus in accented English and the rest of the lyrics in Amharic.

Just as the second chorus was beginning, every light in the theater suddenly went dark. The crowd stood in inquisitive silence for a moment, thinking that perhaps this was part of the grand finale. But when the band stopped playing as well, the crowd began screaming, and the center descended into chaos.

The power was out for only twenty seconds before The Mechanic switched the master power switch back into the "on" position. The lights slowly began to brighten, revealing to the crowd that every single member of The Scheming Lemurs had vanished from the stage.

MisterLemur.com/CT171

- Hear the song *Yes I Can* performed by Selam Alem

Chapter 53: Rodents?

People were running everywhere when Selam tapped the microphone in a largely futile attempt to get everyone's attention. "*I'm afraid the time is now gone. So we will say 'Goodnight.' We thank you for your support! Goodnight!*"

As Selam stepped off the stage, The Mechanic appeared out of the commotion. He grabbed her roughly by the arm, hissing "Where did those furry little rodents go?"

She looked at him blankly. "Rodents?"

He locked eyes with her, gauging her sincerity for a moment, before pushing her away and continuing his search.

Chapter 54: The Back Window

The next light I saw came from the dashboard of a darkened van as it pulled away from The Jameson Center. Selam and her band were sharing a hardy laugh as they unbuckled their instrument cases and released their contraband crop of smuggled lemurs (and friends) onto the floor of the rented van.

Through the rear window, we saw flashing police lights and a news camera. We also saw The Mechanic and several of his handcuffed accomplices being placed into the back of police cars.

While most of the other musicians on stage had been receiving instructions on chord changes and tempo, The Scheming Lemurs had also been given instruction on Selam's plan.

Selam explained. "I knew they would not dare kidnap you on stage. That would have been seen by everyone. But after the show, when you were walking from the stage to the getting dressed room . . ." She shook her head gravely. "You had to escape before the music ended.

"At first, I thought about all the bad men who were trying to get you, and I think, 'This is not possible—for me to help you.' Then I laughed at myself and remembered, 'I will always say *I can*; I will never say *I can't*.'

"I saw that you are not so big and that we could smuggle you away in our instrument cases . . . if it was possible to put you into these cases without everyone seeing what had been done. And when I saw Lava, I knew that he could turn off the power switch without anyone noticing."

Lava sat on the top of the gear shift with a big grin. He stopped smiling only when he had to leap to avoid being squished when the driver quickly applied his hand to shift gears.

Selam turned serious: "Now what?"

"To the Cape Town airport. With any luck, we'll have a plane waiting for us there."

175

Chapter 55: Why?

When we pulled into the private plane section of the Cape Town International Airport, Captain Aye-Aye and Jenny had the plane gassed-up and ready to go.

"Selam, thank you so much. We look forward to seeing you in Sydney!"

She smiled. "So, I have to ask. Why were those men trying to hurt you?"

I scratched the back of my lemur head. "We don't know. From the time we started this Rivals in Rhyme competition, back in Madagascar, it seems like someone's been out to get us. We've been trying to figure it out for months, and we can't."

Selam smiled again. "I will always say 'I can'; I will never say 'I can't.'"

Foosana stuck her head out of the plane. "Come on! Let's get out of here! They probably didn't arrest ALL of The Mechanic's goons!"

I gave Selam a hug and bounded up the boarding stairs two at a time, closing and locking the door of *The Screaming Lemur* behind me.

The sun was just beginning to rise when we touched down on Ranomafana's dirt airstrip.

Chapter 56: Closure

I'd been too excited to sleep for most of the flight home, and dozed off only for the last two hours.

We all piled into a taxi when we landed, and I requested a detour. I knew Tambo's widow Manda Lin was an early riser, and that she'd be sitting on the patio sipping tea, just as she did every morning. Our success would make her happy, and I still had not had the chance to offer my condolences after Tambo's passing.

As we suspected, she was sitting quietly when our taxi pulled up in front of her house. She was alone, and unsurprisingly, she was surprised to see us.

I held it together until I got to the screen door and then burst out crying. I gave her a big hug.

"Are you okay?" she asked.

"We just advanced to the hemisphere finals!" I sobbed, "But I wish Tambo could have been there to see it!"

Manda Lin hugged me tightly. "I know he wishes he had been there, too. Sometimes life is like that. He knew you would be successful."

I reached into the pocket of my blue overalls and pulled out a folded piece of paper. It was her note. "I want you to know," I sniffed, "that we used his advice in the contest. I am going to keep this with me . . . forever."

I handed Manda Lin the note. She opened it and read it slowly. Then she read it again.

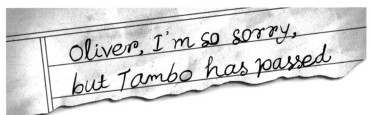

A smile crept over her face. "Then you will want to keep the rest of the note, too. Do you have the rest of the note?"

"The rest of the note?"

"Yes, there was more to the note when I wrote it."

I looked at Numbat. He thought for a moment.

"Wait! Yeah! I, oh . . ." he paused sheepishly. Then he glanced at me. "So, there was this mongo bowl of totally delicious looking chips just kickin' it on the table when we rolled in. It was, you know, right after we bounced outta' camp for the day, and those chips totally tickled my fancy. I was ready to grub down, but I was chomping on some gum. I saw a piece of paper on the table, and tore off part of the paper to put my gum in."

We all stared at him.

"I think I stuffed the paper—and the gum—under the couch . . . right over . . ." He took a few steps and lowered himself onto the floor. ". . . HERE!" he reached under the couch and pulled out a folded piece of paper with a wad of bubblegum squished inside. Then he handed it to me. Yuck.

I accepted it reluctantly, and unfolded it. Then I began reading it aloud. "a kidney stone, and we had to take him to the doctor. Come see us again soon!"

Then I put the two pieces of the note together and read them again.

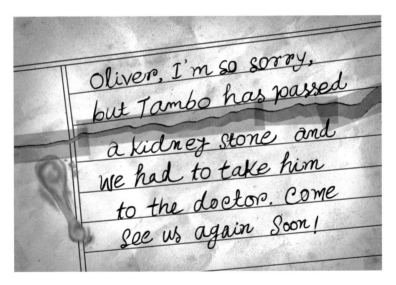

Oliver, I'm so sorry, but Tambo has passed a kidney stone and we had to take him to the doctor. Come see us again Soon!

My eyes practically popped out of my head. "So, so, you mean Tambo is not dead?"

"Oh goodness, no. He's not even that sick anymore. He's at The VBC getting ready to open this morning. Go see him. He'll be very excited to talk with you all!"

Chapter 57: The VBC

Manda Lin must have called ahead, because when we arrived, there was a big sign in front of The VBC saying "Congratulations, Scheming Lemurs!"

We practically ran into the cafe, where we were greeted with a booming, "Power Clap for The Scheming Lemurs on three! One. . .

Two. . . Three!" from more than fifty people crowded inside. I gave Tambo a huge hug.

"You're alive!" I cried. Tears stood in my eyes.

"With apologies to Samuel Clemens, er, Mark Twain, it seems that reports of my 'passing' WERE greatly . . . truncated," Tambo laughed heartily.

With that, everyone roared with laughter and hugged each other happily. Even Captain Aye-Aye lifted a cup of coffee in cheer. Just then the stereo kicked on, and we all started dancing. What a deliriously happy way to begin the day.

I had to tickle myself to make sure I wasn't dreaming.

~ The End ~

Truncated: shortened as if having a part cut off; cut short

About the Author

Oliver *"Mister"* Lemur is a ring-tailed lemur. He moved to Madagascar's Ranomafana National Park when he was very young. He lives there with his parents, his sister, "Pup," and his dog Henry. Oliver attends Namorana Elementary School, and plays the bass guitar. In addition to his native Lemur language, Oliver speaks English and French.

Oliver journals regularly and the notes from his journal (and his friends' journals) played a key role in his retelling of this adventure. This is book two in The Scheming Lemurs series.

OTHER WORKS

BOOKS

- ❖ MISTER LEMUR'S TRAIN OF THOUGHT
  Gold Medal for Children's Poetry, 2011 Moonbeam Awards
  (a collection of 66 of Mister Lemur's rhymes). Grades 2-5
- ❖ IT WILL TAKE A LOT OF US TO LIFT A
  HIPPOPOTAMUS (32 pages). Grades Pk – 2
- ❖ THE SANTA CLAUS ALARM (by Lemur Pup –
  Mister Lemur's little sister) (32 pages) Grades Pk – 2
- ❖ THE SCHEMING LEMURS; RIVALS IN
  RHYME (144 pages) Grades 2-5

MUSIC

- ❖ Adventures in Your Head (music album)
- ❖ Adventures in Writing Camp: You Won't
  Believe Where Writing Will Take You!
- ❖ Adventures in Writing Camp: What Could
  Be Better?
- ❖ Adventures in Writing Camp: What Kind of
  Writer Are You?

All books and music can be purchased at
www.TheLemurStore.com. A portion of sales is
donated to causes supporting the protection of
lemurs and/or lemur habitat.

STARING CONTEST
By Mister Lemur

Today my goldfish looked at me
and gurgled out, "I think
that if we had a staring war
you'd be the first to blink."

I had not cleaned his bowl in days
which caused me to surmise
that the algae growth inside his bowl
would irritate his eyes.

I yelled, "You've got a challenge, Fish!"
Then certain I would win,
I counted down from three to one,
and hollered out, "Begin!"

There's not much to the "play-by-play"
in any staring war.
He stared at me. I stared at him
'til I could stare no more.

I yelped, "Let's make it best of three."
I whispered, "Best of seven?"
Before I won a single match...
..."Best of one-eleven?"

He beat me fifty-six straight times,
and then he smiled, "I think
it's time that someone told you that
a goldfish cannot blink.

"We fish can never blink our eyes.
We have no lids at all...
which means the odds that I blink first
are really, really small!"

So when you're playing with your pets,
make sure the games you choose,
are games that neither one of you
is guaranteed to lose!

MAYHEM IN THE AM
By Mister Lemur

There's mayhem in the AM
in our humble family home.
My little sister spilled the soap.
We're ankle deep in foam.

Our cat brought us a mouse she caught.
Our dog was stung by bees.
Grandma won't stop coughing
like she's got Black Lung Disease.

The cereal is on the floor.
There's jelly in my hair.
I put my pants on inside out
beneath my underwear.

The TV's turned up way too loud.
We can't find our remote.
I need to leave to go to school
but I can't find my coat.

And when I ran to catch the bus,
I slipped in all the suds,
and tumbled head-first down the stairs
with bumps and clunks and thuds.

But mom says, "I won't trade the mess,
the bees, the noise, the foam.
This mayhem in the AM
is what makes our house a home."

Hans and Jen Hartvickson have been creating stories and music together since 2010. They chose "Mister Lemur" as their pen-name after falling in love with lemurs during a trip to Madagascar.

Hans and Jen were inspired to write by their mothers, who are both retired teachers. They are blessed to work with a wonderful team of musicians, artists, teachers and friends to bring Mister Lemur to the world. They spend their summers helping elementary school students become authors at Mister Lemur's Adventures in Writing Camp. www.AIWcamp.com.

Hans has been writing since the first grade. He loves sharing the fun of rhyming stories with kids of all ages. Hans holds a bachelor's degree in Economics from Stanford University and an M.B.A. from The University of Pennsylvania's Wharton School.

Jen travels the country speaking to schools, art associations and after school programs about the importance of writing, setting goals, and making plans. She earned a bachelor's degree in Sociology and a master's degree in Education from Stanford University.